Blood Ties

Also by Pauline Bell in Macmillan:

The Dead Do Not Praise

Feast Into Mourning

No Pleasure in Death

The Way of a Serpent

Downhill to Death

Sleeping Partners

A Multitude of Sins

Pauline Bell

Blood Ties

MACMILLAN

First published 1998 by Macmillan
an imprint of Macmillan Publishers Ltd
25 Eccleston Place, London SW1W 9NF
and Basingstoke

Associated companies throughout the world

ISBN 0 333 72806 8

1 3 5 7 9 8 6 4 2

A CIP catalogue record for this book is available from
the British Library.

Phototypeset by Intype London Ltd
Printed and bound in Great Britain by
Mackays of Chatham plc, Chatham, Kent

For Tracie

Prologue

1942

The siren's wail grew from a murmur to a deafening crescendo as a breathless girl beat on Dorothy Greenhow's door. 'Connie's started,' she gasped, then, duty done, conscience clear, she dashed away to the safety of the air-raid shelter.

When the raids had been an unfamiliar danger, it had cost Dorothy a struggle to respond to a night call whilst her neighbours, supervised by reassuring wardens, filed safely into their gloomy dugout to play dominoes and gossip until it was all over. Now, two years on, like everyone, she was convinced that she would be one of the survivors. Despite blood and death and absurdity she contemplated her own future with certainty.

Not that she despised the shelters. It was interesting underground. You met all sorts down there. Scottish Presbyterians sat next to drunkards. In fact lifestyles were indicated by what was drunk there: rum, cocoa, herb tea or meths – all out of teacups. She watched the last of the crowd of her neighbours and friends drifting calmly along as the wail died away. The road was becoming deserted. A police car sped past the junction. Their sheep safely in the fold, the wardens calmly began to take up their stations. During the day, normal life was real and war and bombs a fantasy. During a raid, it was the other way round.

Dorothy shook herself back to her immediate situation. The government's mass call-up of women for war work had led, in her own district at least, to an unprecedented outbreak of pregnancies as a way out of the factories. It was high time she attended to the conclusion of this one. She picked up her gas mask and dropped it on top of the delivery bag in the pannier of her bicycle and mounted, reflecting sadly on the inexorable fate of the child she was about to deliver. Connie's drinking had led to her other two children spending much of their short lives in foster homes. How long would it be before the authorities took this one into care too?

The barrage balloon was iridescent in the moonlight that made Dorothy's ride through the blackout easier than usual. At the crossroads, two old men were self-importantly fire-watching. She smiled to herself at the huge poster she knew was plastered on the wall above them. It was too dark to see it now but she had read it many times in daylight. IS YOUR JOURNEY REALLY NECESSARY? As she pedalled, she prayed that a helpful neighbour would have collected Connie's government maternity pack with its rubber sheet and brown paper. She certainly wouldn't have done it for herself. Still, Dorothy could improvise. She'd done it before.

Her heart sank as she approached the house. The

voice, strong and surprisingly tuneful, floated through the door that stood open on to the street.

'You are my sunshine, my only sunshine,
You make me happeee . . . when skies are grey.
You'll never know deeear, how much I love you . . .'

Fortunately, the lights were all out. Dorothy climbed off her bicycle and lifted it carefully over the smashed bottle on the pavement and into the house. She closed the door, drew the blackout curtains across, switched on the light, then went outside to check that none was escaping. Satisfied, she slipped through the door again and surveyed the scene.

More bottles, this time intact, lay about a room that had not seen a broom in weeks. Connie, sprawled on a stained and unsavoury sofa, stopped singing and began to whimper. Dorothy lifted her patient's skirt and found no knickers impeding her examination. Still only two fingers dilated. There was time yet. She asked, 'Where's your maternity pack?' Connie's expression was faintly puzzled. Dorothy raised her voice and shook the woman's shoulder. 'Pack!'

The whimpering stopped and Connie beamed, ready to offer her best effort.

'Pack up your troubles in your old kitbag
And smile, smile, smile . . .'

Dorothy shrugged and joined in the rendering to encourage herself as she went through to the slop kitchen and set water to boil. She could hear planes overhead but as yet no explosions.

There was no way she was going to be able to get Connie on to her bed upstairs. She might as well stay handy to the disgusting kitchen. Unceremoniously, she pulled the sofa cushions from under the distended body and made a bed on the floor. She covered it with rubber and cotton sheets of her own, less to protect the cushions from the mess of the birth than to protect the baby from the revolting cushions. Having dragged Connie, with some difficulty, on to the improvised bed, Dorothy slipped into her usual routine. Several songs and many howls and curses later, she delivered a healthy male child with red hair. Connie was brunette. Goodness knew who the father was.

Dorothy cuddled and admired the squirming baby and wondered what to do with him. The two town hospitals were bursting at the seams and there was no way he could be left with his mother, now as clean and comfortable as Dorothy could make her in the circumstances and snoring loudly. Till the raid was over, all she could think of was to take him home with her. She stacked her equipment away and leaned her bicycle against the wall outside. Then she fashioned a sling out of two muslin nappies from her case, knotted at the corners, and manoeuvred herself into it. With her thick coat buttoned round it for extra support and warmth, it would make the infant a safe enough carrier for the short journey.

As she set off, Dorothy saw the raid in the middle distance. Four bombs fell, flash, boom! Sparks and debris shot up into the air four times in quick succession, and, in the sky overhead, an enormous, satanic sunset appeared. Further along her route, shop windows had shattered. In places, the road was thick with glass and the air with dust. As she neared home, she saw two houses down in the next street to hers and people digging for bodies. Beside them, in a crater, a burst water main spouted. Usually, if she passed such a situation, she stopped to offer first aid. Tonight, she had another charge.

She was thankful, though not surprised, to find her fire still glowing. Sprinkling each scuttleful of coal with salt water and washing soda really did make it burn more slowly. The baby, though, must not be placed near it, in danger from little domestic explosions from the shale that made up most folks' coal ration.

Within an hour of his birth, the child was sleeping sweetly in the bottom drawer of her bureau, warm and comfortable in a nest of clean towels and tea cloths. Though deeply weary, Dorothy still, from long habit, re-sterilized her instruments before she made herself a pot of tea. There was no knowing how soon they'd be needed again.

She was no longer in the mood for dominoes and cocoa. She would spend the rest of the night in her own bed, the improvised cradle beside it, and abandon herself to her fantasies. The dreaded yellow envelope had never come. Ray wasn't missing, believed dead. He wasn't even abroad. He'd just gone downstairs to prepare a feed for this new first son of theirs. The child's hair was black, like Ray's. That ginger glint was a trick of the light . . .

She was rudely awakened by a further beating on her door. In a fog, she groped her way to it, clutching a bedjacket to veil the neckline of her substantial nightdress. The door opened to reveal a warden, Sid from next door but one. His mouth moved as she tried to drag herself back to full consciousness. Behind him, she could see incendiaries falling, small and pretty like fireflies. Easy to put out if you found them immediately. A plane could carry thousands of them. She blinked and concentrated on Sid's mouth.

He was reproachful. 'You're wanted. I've wasted time looking in the shelter for you . . .'

'Where?'

Sid gestured. 'Lady Muck! Up at Spencer Lodge.'

Dorothy shook her head. 'She isn't on my list. She'll be booked in at the nursing home. Anyway, she isn't due for another two months.' Then, more urgently, 'She isn't hurt, is she . . .?'

Sid cut her off in her turn. 'No ambulances. Incendiaries started a big fire up at High Clough. They're all there – and she's bleeding bad. You'd better get up there.' He waited and saw her to the end of the road before returning to his post.

Dorothy knew Alice from the Lodge. It had been at her invitation that Dorothy had begun to teach first aid to St Matthew's WI. That was how they had come to be on first-name terms and how Dorothy had come to know quite a lot about her. She had soon realized that Alice and her two particular friends were the only ones who really would wade in and get their hands bloodied when the call came, and she had been right. She had a lot of time for Alice who was thirty-two now, and had a history of miscarriages. Dorothy vowed to save this baby if it were humanly possible.

It wasn't. Alice was very frightened and in great pain. She had bled profusely and the baby, a breach presentation, refused to budge. Dorothy soothed her patient and gave her as much gas and air as she dared before slashing at the vaginal wall to hurry the delivery. The child arrived, dark-haired, female and dead.

As soon as Dorothy had taken hold of the little body she had known it was too late, but she nevertheless slapped it vigorously and dunked it alternately in very hot and very cold water for what seemed like hours. Then she placed it on the bed beside its mother and wept, for Alice, for the baby, for herself, for Ray.

On his last leave they had gone to a nightclub in Leeds and a bomb had fallen on one end of the dance floor, killing all the band except the drummer. They had been dancing to 'Oh, Johnny!' when the place was hit. The couples at the band end of the hall had stood for some seconds as if still dancing, then leaned and fallen dead. The young were killed and the old survived! Good mothers had stillbirths and drunken prostitutes had healthy babies!

Alice, in an uneasy doze, wrinkled her nose as limp strands of dark hair tickled it. Her beloved Jack, away in the Navy, but smiling from his photograph frame on the bedside table, had a chestnut thatch. Dorothy was filled with a sudden fury. Why shouldn't she play God? She couldn't make a worse mess of His world than He seemed to be doing Himself!

Chapter One

1997

Jon Parker slammed the kitchen door with as much force as his slight frame could manage in combat with sixteen square feet of solid hardwood. He cleared the steep flight of stone steps in one bound. The soles of his new trainers safely gripped the icy cobbles of the back-street as he took furious flight from his unjust accuser.

He ignored the frantic braking of the car that was reversing into the alley from the backyard at the end of the row and cut across its path, oblivious of the driver's curses and the neighbours' lifted curtains. He was not upset, he told himself bitterly. He was angry. He had every right to be angry.

For a while, he gloried in his anger, as it supplied his breakfastless body with energy to run and the warmth to compensate for his forgotten jacket. Then, breathless, he slowed down and began to plan his revenge. Some of the passers-by, hurrying to work, recognized him and greeted him, trying to catch his eye. They were met with that hooded-eyed, expressionless mask that passed for cool in certain of Cloughton's streets.

*

From her kitchen doorstep, Beryl Parker looked down the hill at descending terraces of houses. The occupants of the nearest had an unrestricted view into her basement from their living rooms and into her own living room from their bedrooms. There was little that she could hide from them about the events that made up her family's day.

She had never really resented their non-malicious scrutiny and, perhaps, now she could turn it to her advantage. The resounding slam of the door on Jonathan's departure would not have failed to alert their attention. Careful questions might elicit the direction in which he had run, without giving too much away.

She shivered and went back indoors. The cartoon drawing lay on the table. It both fascinated and repelled her. Jonathan was no artist and the pictures were crudely drawn. There were six of them in two rows but it was the fifth one that had burned itself into her mind. She picked up the paper, forced herself to re-examine it.

The sheet had been intended for a piece of work set by one of his tutors, fairly neatly headed with yesterday's date and the row of initials he was so proud of, P. N. J. Parker, both underlined. She could think of nothing that had happened the previous evening that might have upset him, diverted him from the assignment he'd been about to tackle and set him instead on the frenzied drawing, its heavy pencil lines here and there tearing the paper.

The actual events that the scenes depicted had been gradually fading from her conscious memory.

From her son's too, she had hoped. She knew he blamed her for all the trouble. She blamed herself too, to a certain extent, had admitted as much to him, though he'd given her no credit for that, made no allowance for her own unhappiness. She believed most of the trouble he'd been in since had been, at least in part, to punish her, but they'd been getting on better since he began on this course. He'd made some attempt to see things from her side. And so this morning, finding the sketches had greatly upset her.

She had taken them, at first, to be further provocation, but supposing they had been an attempt on his part to remove his offence from his conscience, a sudden urge to transfer it to a piece of paper which he could throw away and be rid of? She wondered what might have been the title of the piece of work he'd intended to begin when he'd headed the sheet. His tutor would have received a shock if Jon had handed in what was on it now.

When she had seen it, laid out on the breakfast table to attract her attention, she had weighed into him furiously. Her own words seemed to echo round the room now, though when she had spoken them, they had not. Words had no chance to echo in the poky space. Now she feared she had been wrong to be angry. Maybe it had all been preying on his mind.

She sank into an armchair and tears somehow found a way out of her closed eyes. How dared he, she'd finally demanded, make fun of an action that had lost her her last chance of getting her daughter, his sister, back? Her angry outburst had probably doubled the shame and blame he might have been suffering.

Stephanie was a tease, had been since she was a tiny girl. Jonathan had a temper over which he'd gained little mastery even now, five years on. On the occasion of the assault, though, their quarrel had had more specific causes. Jon's father had welcomed his daughter but rejected him, and Stephanie, neither sensitive nor considerate, had enjoyed her triumph.

Beryl swallowed and picked up the sheet of paper yet again. Did the positions of the two figures in the fifth little box indicate sexual assault? Jonathan had not been accused of this officially and she had never dared to ask him. Maybe the balloon of heavily scored question marks coming out of the male figure's head meant that even Jon himself hadn't been sure of his intentions.

She wondered what she should do now. It was likely that he'd have run to his friends, that he was planning, with them, to get into further trouble. Maybe she should ring Highfield House and say that he was ill. If he failed to show up with no excuse offered, he'd be off his course and back in court. But what if he'd come to his senses and decided to attend? What would the staff make of her attempt to cover for him?

She refused to examine her worst fear, that, with the assault of his sister still preying on his unstable mind, he might have gone to his father's house and been goaded to repeat the attack. Should she ring Barry and warn him? She hesitated to do that. There had been signs, recently, that the breach between Jon and his father's new family had been healing. She'd be destroying the possibility of civilized relations in the future. She couldn't put that in jeopardy. She dropped the paper back on the table. She was sure, almost, that Jon wouldn't hurt Steff again.

Judging by the way he had slammed out of the house, though, she doubted very much that he had been on his way to 'college'. She hardly thought of it now in inverted commas. She had accepted the polite fiction herself along with the neighbours it was meant to deceive. She dried her eyes, then filled the kettle to make fresh tea. She didn't want it but her mind worked better when her hands were busy.

Jon's track record suggested she wouldn't see him for a day or two. She was not worried that he would be short of somewhere to sleep, the loan of clean clothes or offers of food, even though he had left empty-handed and minus his jacket. He had plenty of friends who would provide for him, but only on condition that he reverted to his gang membership, joined in their plans and got into more trouble. The tears began again as she cursed her too ready tongue.

Who would he be most likely to go to? None of his acquaintances seemed to go by more than a forename, or, more often, a nickname. She had ignored them, not wanting to encourage them or get to know them. She knew now that this had not been wise.

As she poured water into the teapot she debated the wisdom of phoning the probation officer. He was certainly the most understanding and helpful of the probation officers Jonathan had had, but she'd be putting him in a moral dilemma, making him choose between betraying Jon or breaking his contract with the court.

She put down her untasted tea. She would be sick if she tried to swallow anything. Could Jon possibly have run to some girl, up to his father's tricks, maybe? She shook her head, reprimanded herself. It wasn't a crime to have a girlfriend, for goodness' sake, if, like Jon, you were free, unattached. In fact, a nice girl might be the making of him, someone to care about besides himself, someone he was free to love because he hadn't stored up a million grudges against her to be a barrier between them.

As Beryl Parker finally picked up the phone to offer fictitious excuses for her son's absence from Highfield House, her eyes stared, unseeing, at the chimney pots of a terraced row some fifty yards further down the hill. In one of its houses, in the front, slightly larger and therefore 'main' bedroom, Denis Betts, vicar's warden of St Barnabas' Church, Cloughton, suddenly woke to find the low winter sun illuminating the carefully embroidered flowers on his pillowcase and dazzling his eyes.

He shaded them and peered at the clock. Seven forty-five! He had meant to be up two hours ago. Groaning softly to himself with vexation and slight malaise, he swung his legs out of bed and sat up. His feet made contact with icy linoleum and the chill shock completed the waking-up process. Grabbing dressing gown and groping with his toes for slippers, he made his way first to the bathroom (minute), and then to the kitchen (almost as minute), seeing their size – or lack of it – in his present circumstances as an advantage. His wife had decreed that this first of his three weeks' annual holiday should be spent on a wholesale redecoration of the house.

He had agreed to the plan as meekly as he had agreed with his employer's reasons for assigning to him this unpopular time for the taking of leave. 'A lot to be said, Betts, after the frenzy of Christmas and New Year, for packing the kids back to school and enjoying a few days' peace.' Denis forbore to mention that his children, aged two and a half and four, had not yet reached that convenient stage.

He and the pair of them had spent two on the whole enjoyable days respectively stripping the walls of the house's five tiny rooms and romping in the resultant exciting heaps of paper sculpture. The infants' pleasure had been tempered by their mother's groans about the state of their garments, and Denis's by the recurrence of vague symptoms that had troubled him, on and off, for some months. Sudden abdominal pains, vague in situation at the beginning of the attack, tended to settle in a day or two in a spot just inside his right hip bone. Yesterday he'd felt rather sick, had no appetite, but working through lunchtime had at least gained his wife's commendation.

In the evening, the stripping of walls and preparation of woodwork being completed, she had borne off young Gary and Emma to her mother's house so that the contents of pots of paint and buckets of paste could be spread where they were needed and nowhere else. She had left early so that the children would be established in Grandmother's house by their usual bedtime.

Denis had promised himself a night out with the boys between the comparatively destructive and constructive parts of his task, but when the time had arrived he had not felt up to it. His symptoms were not likely, he had reluctantly admitted to himself, to be improved by the administration of beer. Instead, he had lain on a settee that was covered in dust sheets and watched televised football. Still uncomfortable after an evening's relaxation, he had visited the off-licence to purchase medicinal brandy. After a substantial dose he had fallen into bed and slept immediately, only to wake in the small hours, tossing and turning. He began a fitful doze towards five-thirty, just minutes before he had intended to rise.

After he had washed and dressed, he felt marginally better. He'd be fine in another hour or two. He always had been before. He carried his modest breakfast over to the chair by the fire, taking a childish pleasure in the unusual echoing sounds that bounced off the bare walls and floors.

He found the dun colour of the scraped walls was more restful to the eye than the paper that had been covering them, certainly than the new ones his wife had selected. He shuddered as he unwound the beginning of a roll intended for this room, then shrugged and carried his breakfast dishes to the sink.

He planned the day's work as he washed and dried them. First coat on all the woodwork this morning, and he'd begin with the bathroom. It was the smallest, and having one under his belt would make him feel he was getting on. If he finished early enough, he'd try to call in on old Mr Oliver later this afternoon.

He felt he ought to have a word with the vicar about him on Sunday. The old chap really couldn't go on living alone. Denis had found a gas tap on and the ring not lit last time he'd called. He'd mentioned it to the daughter but she didn't seem to be doing anything about it. The Reverend Tony Kirkbride would soon get things moving though. Denis folded the drying cloth and popped the tray of clean crockery under the dust sheet on the table. Right, now for the bathroom.

Suddenly he began to shiver uncontrollably as an icy chill gripped him. His stomach muscles cramped and his hands, automatically drawn to the source of pain, felt a hard, unyielding surface that seemed not to be soft flesh. He collapsed into the fireside chair and lay back, his knees drawing themselves up without his volition.

He could no longer bear his hands touching his abdominal region and he removed them to his perspiring face. He could hear his own breathing, rapid and shallow, using only his chest muscles. The pain increased sickeningly and he vomited profusely. Even *in extremis*, he felt thankful that the chair was protected by a double thickness of dust sheet. Then, fear of his own imminent demise swamped even his fear of Irene's wrath over a stained and malodorous chair.

After some minutes, he became dimly aware of a hammering at the door. He was incapable of rising to open it but managed a feeble call. The rapping continued, till, suddenly and mercifully, the door, improperly latched and opening directly on to the street, swung inwards. A further bleated 'Help!' brought the postman hurrying inside, still clutching the parcel he was trying to deliver.

Denis drifted in and out of consciousness. Through a haze of pain, he was unsure whose hands lifted him on to a stretcher, whose voice murmured, 'Temp. 105'. Certainly, he was unaware that the patient disgorged from the ambulance arriving in the bay outside Casualty simultaneously with his own was Dorothy Greenhow, the midwife who had delivered him and, over a period of more than thirty years, possibly twenty per cent of all Cloughton's babies.

He was the more acutely but she the more gravely ill.

Forty-eight hours earlier, the Reverend Anthony Kirkbride had accompanied Irene Betts to Cloughton General Hospital and had looked down with her on a patient who was unconscious and seriously ill. Now he was delighted but not unduly surprised to see that same patient, his warden, Denis Betts, sitting up against a heap of pillows and seeming to be in something approaching his usual health.

He took a deep breath before going through the door of the four-bedded ward and ran a finger between his clerical collar and the damp skin at the back of his neck. The three patients within were dressed - or rather undressed - to suit the temperature. And, having been here for more than an hour or two, they were inured to the threatening antiseptic smell.

Glancing round, Tony could see nothing to sit on, and considered fetching a chair before deciding against it. Hospital chairs, surely specifically designed to be cumbersome and uncomfortable, were invariably stacked at the wrong end of the ward for the bed occupied by his visitee. Had he just coined a word, he wondered?

According to Irene, who seemed to have visited her husband just once in the two days, Denis needed to speak to him urgently. He knew that a gulf separated his own from his warden's definition of urgency, but he was fond of this earnest young man whose conscientious work in the parish considerably lightened his own burden of responsibility.

He approached the bed and dropped his offerings on the foot of it, before handing them to the patient one by one. 'Holly and Christmas roses from the vicarage garden, from Jean, of course. Miniatures of brandy and whisky from me - a convenient size for concealment, yet sufficient for present needs. There's a card signed by all the choirboys and a book of chess problems from Cavill. Looks as though you won't need that, though.'

Tony nodded towards the locker top where a half-completed game was set out. 'You obviously found a fellow enthusiast. Is he any good?'

'He's brilliant. He's gone for his physio just now.

Tell Cavill thanks, I'll need the book to learn a few new tricks.'

'So, how are you?'

Denis grinned. 'Fine. A bit tired of being told I'm a lucky man and being lectured on – you know . . .'

'The stupidity of ignoring recurring symptoms? They're right, you know. You can still die of peritonitis if you don't report in for your op and your antibiotics. You still look a bit washed out, even with them. I told Jean you would be. Managed to leave her behind. Not a time to have women around, is it, when you're *hors de combat*? Gives them the upper hand. Jean wants to do her best for the whole world, bless her, but you have to be strong enough to stand it. Wasn't it Lewis who said about someone that he devoted his life to helping others and that you could tell the others by the hunted looks on their faces?'

Denis looked wistful. 'Could you explain that to Irene? Tell her I'm only strong enough for male company?' They both laughed, though neither was amused.

'Jean's brilliant with some of the old folk.' Tony had managed to relieve some of his warden's guilt at his lack of enthusiasm for his wife's company, but felt that he perhaps owed a mental apology to his own wife.

Denis sat forward. 'That's what I wanted to see you about.' He launched into the convoluted story of old Mr Oliver of Saxby Street, his gas taps and his daughter. 'The last time I went round, it was five o'clock teatime, and the old chap was just getting up, convinced it was early morning. And he can't remember things. I'd called only a couple of days before and he swore blind no one had been near him for three weeks.'

Tony promised to attend to things, noting that their few minutes' conversation had already wearied the patient. As he took his leave, he remembered that Jean had offered to mind the Betts' children that evening so that Irene could visit again. He wondered if he could somehow upset these arrangements and save his warden from thirty minutes of thinly veiled reproaches on the subject of unfinished wallpapering.

Having completely lost track of the television play she had been watching, Jean Kirkbride switched off the set and took up her copy of *Woman and Home*. The phone had been ringing ever since Tony had returned from visiting Denis Betts, and a list of messages in her neat script bore witness to its ringing all the time he had been out. She had not been surprised, therefore, that he had had to go out again, but she was disappointed that it was old Mr Oliver that he had currently gone to see.

She was well aware of the parish's antipathy to her ministrations, and had the sense, when people specifically asked for her husband, to let him deal with them. They considered Jean to be no better than themselves, worse in fact for having married out of her class. Let no one say the class system in Britain was breaking down. Jean was found wanting. She could offer them neither the magic wand of a university education, nor the reassurance of a high-bred accent and an authoritative manner.

The old folk though were her forte, and she felt a little slighted by Tony's interference. She would have thought old Mr O. would have preferred her cheerful, practical help to Tony's charm. Still, she had been touched by her husband's wanting her to be spared going out in such filthy weather until it occurred to her that he might be worried about his car. Her slight pique was not mitigated by her own fear that, by proceeding overcautiously on wet, dark roads, she might provoke another driver to behave rashly.

She suspected that Mr Oliver's dementia was politically motivated. She stood no nonsense from him and he never forgot her own visits, nor any of the promises she made to do things for him. She ought to talk to him very soon, and severely too. That game with the gas taps might be very effective in getting him the attention he craved but it was extremely dangerous.

She couldn't have been bothered to argue with him tonight though. In fact she was glad to have her feet up. The Betts children were sweet and well disciplined – over-disciplined in Jean's opinion, at least by their mother – but they were lively and she was not a young woman any more. She had come home feeling exhausted.

Her magazine failed to hold her attention. She had read it through once already and she was pleased when the phone rang again. She liked chatting to friends and even people who really wanted Tony were quite happy to trust her with messages. Her heart sank when Tony's sister greeted her.

The mere sound of Diana's voice made Jean feel fat and frumpy. She knew just what was intended when Diana said how pleased she was that her brother faced every task with such a stout supporter. She looked down at her folds of flesh, draped unbecomingly with more folds of faded woollen dressing gown. Tony said Diana's disdain was all in Jean's mind, and, in her cheerful moments, she believed him. Somehow, she didn't feel very cheerful tonight.

Diana would like to come over for the day on Sunday. Would that be convenient? Mother would come too, of course. Jean was not sure which she dreaded most, visiting Diana or being visited by her. Marginally, home ground was more bearable. In the vicarage she could create diversions, retreat to the kitchen, attend to urgent parish matters. Usually, on their Sunday visits, Tony would give Jean a respite by taking Diana for a walk in the afternoon.

Mrs K. Senior didn't accompany them, of course. Walking more than a few hundred yards was too much for her these days. Still, she found her mother-in-law less intimidating when Diana was absent. The old lady really did appreciate Jean's efforts both to entertain her guests and to be a good wife to her son, even if she would have preferred him to have married someone more attractive, more elegant, altogether more socially suitable.

Jean no longer had aspirations to any of these qualities. She had been a pretty girl once, tall and athletic, but she had been born late in her parents' marriage, their only child. They had lived well into their ninth decade and during the long period of dutiful nursing Jean had found solace in food, both eating it and cooking it expertly and imaginatively for others. Having allowed herself to become a fourteen-stone slab, there seemed little point in doing more than decently covering it.

Perhaps it was time to set the table for Tony's supper. She threw away her chocolate wrappers and replaced her magazine in the rack. There was a shepherd's pie in the oven – her special recipe – and lemon meringue in the fridge. She'd open some wine and let it be warming. Surely Tony wouldn't have to drive off anywhere else tonight.

Chapter Two

Jon Parker pulled the Volvo Estate off the narrow road, into a farm gateway, and sat waiting for his hands and knees to stop shaking. He thought he would never learn to gauge the width of this car. It seemed as if the leafless shrubs that bordered the lane were brushing the front wings on both sides. All lights approaching from the opposite direction threw him into a panic. He'd thought he was going to rip the side off the van he had just passed. He watched its lights disappear over the brow of the hill behind him. As his limbs grew still, he continued to sit, considering his situation.

Ever since he had slammed the door in his mother's face two days ago, he had felt he was being pulled in two different directions. One half of him hated all his relatives. That half was hell-bent on behaving as wildly as he knew – or his present companions could suggest – how, to upset and punish them.

His fellow gang members had turned out not to be all the ones he had expected. Dez and Cracker were still around and up to their old tricks, and Cracker's young brother, Vin. He'd failed to recognize the lad at first but he remembered him now. He was just a bigger version of the same whining hanger-on he'd been before Jon did his three months' stretch for robbery with assault. He hadn't assaulted the stupid woman at all, just fended her off when she'd tried to grab her bag back from him. The rozzers, though, were gunning for him, thought he'd got off too lightly for what he'd given Steff.

Now there was Sola in charge of them all, big and black and bossy, with his double life of street-gang leader and model student, expected to get a brilliant degree and make millions. Jon was sure he'd do just that, probably several millions, whilst all the nobs who were losing them to him thought he was their friend.

Jon hated Sola as much as he hated his mum and his dad and rotten, stuck-up, jammy Stephanie. He hated him more, in fact, because sometimes he didn't hate his family at all. Only when he let himself remember what his mother had said and how his dad had sent him packing and how bloody Steff had laughed.

Nervously, he put the key back in the ignition. He was always going to feel scared of driving this big car that Sola had stolen in Manchester and assigned to him. It was a world away from his mum's Mini and he still didn't feel too confident even driving that. He wasn't sure yet what the job was that Sola was planning, nor why it had to be a Volvo. He wouldn't feel right in it even if he could drive it well – any more than he did in this gear Sola had organized for him to wear. This awful mac had belonged to Dez's *dad*, for goodness' sake. Left to himself, Dez wouldn't have dreamed of offering it but Sola said he had to and even Dez did what Sola said.

Jon sighed, stretched his still quivering arms and wished he were back at Highfield House, free to ask advice from his tutors and Cavill and Rory. Without going back to his mother though, and without Sola being able to find him. He'd like to kill Sola. He'd spoiled everything on the Cloughton streets. Their jobs were no fun any more. Everybody took Sola's orders without question – and without much reward for their pains.

The black bastard came from miles away, somewhere near Brum. Cloughton streets belonged to himself and Dez and Cracker and all the others. Surely, all together, they ought to be able to stand up against Sola, though for the moment he couldn't see it. Unless they could wish him dead. Jon felt that life would be a lot easier if he could wish a lot of people dead.

At Cloughton Royal Infirmary a nurse put her head round the door of the side ward in women's surgical. Was Mrs Greenhow comfortable? Was there anything she'd like? Stupid questions but well meant.

What would she like? Dorothy wondered. Her health and strength back? She didn't think she would really. She had had a good life and a long one. She had had success in a useful career, plenty of excitement, some deep sorrow but much joy and a great satisfaction. She was ready to leave it all now, too tired to go on with it any longer.

Her 'fit' contemporaries were only in wonderful shape 'for their age', their energy diminished, their activities pointless and trivial, their impact on this strange modern world negligible. What Dorothy would like now was dignity, not to go on living but to die a good death.

She'd been wrong to fight against coming in here. She'd thought the doctors would take her over, make decisions for her, take away her independence, talk to her as if she were an imbecile. Hadn't she done as much to others over the years? Always for their own good, of course, and never realizing how patronizing, degrading even, were those conventionally sympathetic encouragements to those whose pain she was not experiencing.

But it hadn't been like that. The doctors had allowed her to accept or refuse their treatment as she chose with no coercion, not even an attempt to persuade. That had told her all she needed to know about her condition. The cancer was widespread, terminal. The little Pakistani, though, had drained her lungs without causing her much extra discomfort. Now she was managing to breathe more easily, to talk normally for short periods until she became too weary.

It wouldn't be long before the fluid collected again of course, and she knew there was a limit to the number of times the miracle could be performed. She would enjoy this respite for a while, just rest against this heap of blissfully soft pillows and gather what strength she could. Very soon now though she would have to drop her bombshell, make her confession, before it was too late.

In a house in a more salubrious part of the town, each of Josephine Merry's paying guests had a private bed-sitting room with adequate furniture and simple cooking facilities. At the beginning of the autumn term, when they had first taken up residence, each had kept to her own quarters, but a chilly autumn and a very cold winter had turned an occasional practice into a common one. On this January evening they took it for granted that they would eat round Jo's pine table, warmed by the Aga and entertained by one another's conversation.

The table having been cleared, Paula and Marianne sat at it and leafed through a slim magazine. Ruth, whose turn it was not, was washing up, seemingly lost in her own thoughts but listening hard.

Paula hooted. 'This one's different.' She read aloud. ' "Older lady? Fancy a spring affair? Very attractive young man, twenty-eight, tall, slim, fit, graduate, professional, creative, sensuous, good company. Seeks older lady (thirty to fifty) with looks, style and intelligence for unforgettable affair." '

Marianne made no reply. Paula continued, undaunted. 'Here's a lefty who lists personal growth as one of his likes.'

Straight-faced, Marianne leaned over to look. 'Well,

he should suit all those women who specify "preferably tall".'

Ruth laughed in spite of her disapproval of their occupation. Realizing that she had been listening, the other two drew her into the conversation and soon they were continuing what had been a long-running argument.

'There's more pressure on a woman to marry than a man. Bachelor isn't insulting like spinster. Nobody puts "old" in front of it.' Paula's tone was defensive, though Ruth had as yet voiced no criticism.

'There's certainly,' Marianne observed, 'no equivalent of "maiden aunt".'

Ruth put the last of the clean dishes into the cupboard and came to sit at the table. 'But there is pressure on some men to be married. Firms like it in their management because of entertaining and so on.'

'Like your James, you mean?' Paula's sidelong glance at Ruth was malicious. Marianne opted out of the conversation and began to write in a notebook. Paula pushed the magazine far enough towards Ruth for her to read it. In spite of herself, Ruth let her eyes follow the print till she became fascinated. Meanwhile, Paula too began to write.

Into the silence, Ruth remarked, 'The terminology's a bit vague. "Likes films" could mean anything, from porno through cartoons to the black and white ones where all the characters jabber unintelligibly and the subtitles slip away before you've finished reading them.' Neither of her companions looked up. 'And how intelligent is intelligent?' Still receiving no reply, she continued to peruse the columns aloud. ' "Upmarket, unpretentious woman graduate". Isn't that a contradiction in terms?'

Tired of being ignored, Ruth obtained the other girls' attention by pulling the magazine away from them and closing it. 'I realize that my asking will inflate your egos to bursting point, but I can't see why either of you should have any trouble finding young men by the conventional method.'

'It's not *young* men we're writing to.'

Marianne's admonitory glance at Paula quickly silenced her. Marianne remarked, equably, 'This method is becoming quite widely accepted.'

Ruth persevered. 'You can't describe yourself in three lines. Words mean different things to different people and you haven't the space to qualify anything.'

'What?'

'Well, if you mention your job, for example, you'll be credited with all the stereotyping that goes with it.'

Five-syllable words were too much for Paula. 'If we had jobs to describe we might not be doing this.' Marianne's usually deadpan face now expressed something akin to fury and Paula hurriedly lightened her tone. 'Can I alter my vital statistics?'

'He's hardly likely to whip out a tape-measure.' Marianne regarded Paula's superfluous stone with distaste before turning back to Ruth. 'We aren't trying to describe ourselves accurately. We're trying to get takers. It's like writing a CV. You just tell a different kind of lie.'

Ruth shrugged and got up to leave the room.

Neither of the other girls asked her to keep their afternoon's activity a secret from Jo but they knew she would say nothing. She was more than a little afraid of Marianne and too soft-hearted to embarrass Paula.

Marianne waited several seconds after the door had closed before turning to Paula. 'You'd better learn to keep your mouth shut.'

'Ruth won't say anything. Anyway, she probably won't be here for much longer. She'll go back to live with her old fuddy-duddy, and then there'll be room here for Briony. You're always saying you need to keep a closer eye on Briony.'

Marianne grinned. 'Maybe Ruth could teach us a thing or two. She got her sugar daddy without working for him.'

Paula's nose wrinkled. 'Yes, but he's expecting her to marry him.'

'She could do worse. After all, she's hardly a bundle of laughs and she's nothing to look at. James is old but he's dishy.'

'Ageing makes a lot of men more attractive, not less.'

'Quite. And James has a well-paid job, big house, expensive car – and he's always buying things for her.'

'Yes, but he's always embarrassing her. Last week she said the waiter at Ginnello's thought he was her father.'

'Lucky Ruth to be eating at Ginnello's.'

'Pr'aps it's not so bad now but what will she do when he's senile?'

Marianne shrugged. 'Then he'll die and she can look for another one.'

By late evening, the rain had stopped. The rising wind had half dried the pavements so that they no longer reflected the palm trees, tropical blossoms and scantily clad beauties depicted in neon tubes on the façade of Cloughton's Caribbean Club. Two girls emerged from this palace of fantasy into the reality of the bleak January night. With practised ease they shook off the two youths who had had hopes of prolonging the evening's pleasures in their company and turned towards home, arm in arm.

Warmth and protection had not been high priorities in their choice of garments, but, at first, they had that careless disregard for the elements that is possible at eighteen. Soon, though, they found strapless bodices, brief skirts and the essential thin black-sequinned jackets inadequate shields against a cruel wind that stiffened their jaws and marred the pleasing lines of their young limbs with goose bumps.

Neither had really enjoyed the evening. It had failed in its purpose in so far as neither had acquired an escort financially or amorously worthy of their long-term attentions. Presently they halted before a small terraced house. Absence of light at the windows told them that parents were abed and older brother had been luckier in his evening's hunting.

The girl whose home this was issued to her companion the hoped-for invitation and they went inside.

'Let's raid their drinks. We bloody need it. See what you fancy in there, Steff, while I look out some glasses.'

After a couple of minutes, Stephanie Parker withdrew her upper body from the sideboard cupboard with brandy in one hand, gin in the other. 'Medicinal, this is.' She had been putting off her request all evening and now decided to delay it further, at least until a couple more drinks had mellowed Katie, made her more amenable.

Katie needed no telling that the wonderful new job had fallen through. What else would account for the absence of gloating? But she too would bide her time.

Soon the level in each bottle had dropped by a couple of inches. The fronts of the girls' alluring legs were marred no longer by goose-flesh but now by scorch marks from the hissing gas fire. Neither girl could remember why they had put off the subject of Stephanie's job.

'Sod their rotten offer, Steff. Bet you decided to turn it down when you heard the whole story.'

Inebriated, Stephanie always told the truth. 'Like hell I did. I'd have jumped at it. Talk about money for jam!' She described the pleasurable duties that would have been required of her and her indignation when she had been found wanting. 'I don't know what I did wrong. I thought I was home and dry. She was actually taking my details, you know, address, bank account number and so on for her accounts, and then she suddenly decided I wouldn't do.'

Katie's solidarity was comforting. 'Well, it's their bloody loss.' Stephanie was ashamed that she had ever doubted her friend's loyalty. 'She probably thought you'd steal her customers.'

Stephanie shook her head. 'She doesn't take any on herself. She just organizes things.'

Katie refilled their glasses. 'Well, my supermarket's still looking for people. It's not much fun and it's not much money but with the mess you're in, at least when you go to court it'll sound better if you can prove you're doing your honest best to get out of debt. And if we both work there it'll be a bit less boring for me.'

It had been a day of squally gusts of rain, alleviated sporadically by cosmetic sunshine. The evening, though, had closed in early even for January and the rain now sliced relentlessly through the near-darkness.

The man could see Briony sitting at the table in the coffee-bar window. Only Cloughton, as far as he knew, had a coffee bar that opened, sixties style, for almost as long as the pubs, and even Cloughton only had the one. She was peering through the glass but she had little hope of picking him out from the surrounding sodden gloom.

He pushed through the door, wrinkling his nose at the smell of wet clothes that masked that of cheap instant coffee. She was prattling at him before he had even reached her table. 'You old dark horse! I'd never have thought it. You could have knocked me down with a feather when—'

'Never mind that. Let's go.'

'What, without even a coffee? The waitress has

been looking daggers at me for the last twenty minutes . . .' The man sighed impatiently. Couldn't she have bought her own coffee for once?

'Yes, I'm sorry. I couldn't get away as soon as I planned.'

She gave him an arch smile. 'Yes, I can just imagine the sort of things that kept you – now! You should have heard what Paula said when I rang up and told her . . .' He turned his sharply indrawn breath into a cough but she had noticed nothing. She was giggling till he pulled her to her feet and towards the door. 'There's no need to be rough – and I'm thirsty.' She pouted.

He endeavoured to be pleasanter. 'We'll find a nice pub and we can have a meal too if you like, but we'll have to drive out somewhere well clear of Cloughton.'

'We will, won't we? Can't have someone seeing us and telling your boss what a naughty boy you are – or your family.'

He smiled sardonically. 'My boss, I'm afraid, knows all about what sort of boy I am.'

'What? You mean you've . . .'

He shook his head impatiently. 'Forget it.' He bundled her into the car. He only wanted sex; she only wanted money. Both admitted that their meetings were for this mutually convenient exchange by the way they dressed for them. She usually wore a respectable blouse or jumper, since an expensive meal was her preferred kind of foreplay, but the preparation of her person was otherwise careless. Tonight her hair was greasy, awaiting the pre-wedding hairdressing appointment most likely arranged for the next morning. His own appearance was hardly smart and trendy. He folded down the collar of the belted gabardine raincoat he was wearing before fastening his seat belt.

She smiled at him uncertainly. 'I wish I hadn't let the oldies stuff me with steak and kidney pie and apple crumble. If I'd known I'd be seeing you tonight, I'd have made some excuse when I arrived, said I'd just had tea or something. I couldn't really do justice to your sort of restaurant tonight.'

He drove on without answering. She had never been comfortable with silence. 'Thank goodness I never have to worry about putting weight on. It'd be a pity to waste your slap-up meals just to keep in shape.' Still he made no reply.

Even she remained silent for some seconds, trying to gauge his strange mood. 'I knew you weren't really called Edward. You often don't answer to it straight away. Well, Marianne said you didn't seem comfortable with it, and then I started to notice she was right.' There was more in the same vein. '... Like I was saying, I was absolutely flabbergasted when ... you know, you really don't look like ...' He kept his eyes on the road, tried to close his mind to it.

When he stopped driving, it was a positive pleasure to encircle her neck with the chain, to pull it hard and squeeze the breath out of her, putting a stop to the stream of inanities, the heavy innuendoes. He was surprised at the strength in his body in the throes of the killing. He'd noticed it last time too, as though a force was inhabiting him, using him temporarily. It began to abate only when she lay still, slumped towards the passenger door. Slowly, it passed from him but it left his mind alert.

He glanced at his watch. He had further plans to make. He'd better dump the body quickly and get away. The allotments would do, in the tangle of blackened shrubs and bracken that filled that one uncultivated plot. Briony would have been grieved to miss being in tomorrow's wedding pictures but he would compensate her by arranging her in the foreground of his tableau when the other girls were ready to join her.

Chapter Three

Jo Merry surveyed her kitchen grimly. A curdled mixture of grease and tomato sauce was congealed on the single plate on the draining board. An oily, red intermittent line ran down the door of the cupboard below where an unmopped spill had dribbled over the edge. A milk carton, left all night out of the fridge, stood on the working surface beside an empty can, a crumpled piece of absorbent kitchen paper and a packet of tipped cigarettes.

Jo had no doubts about which of her lodgers was responsible for the mess. She made herself coffee, sniffing carefully at the suspect milk. Good thing it was January. She had intended, when she'd finished drinking it, to haul Paula out of bed and stand over her until the mess was cleared away. By the time her cup was empty, though, she had decided not to waste time supervising a task that she would have to repeat herself if her exacting standards were to be maintained. Paula was incorrigible. She would just have to go.

Jo shook her head impatiently. Incorrigible was no longer a derogatory word. These days, it was usually spoken with a tolerant smile at the antics of the young and their amusing persistence in antisocial behaviour. She flicked down the kettle's switch and drank a fortifying second cup before getting to work. By the time the telephone rang, all the kitchen surfaces were shining.

'Josephine Merry.'

'Sorry to trouble you. You must be Paula's landlady.' The voice was slightly muffled but definitely male. Jo sighed.

'You can't know Paula very well if you thought it would be her you'd be troubling at this hour on a Saturday morning. I'll get her for you.'

'I trust I didn't interrupt your breakfast. Could you tell her it's Edward?'

Jo forbore to mention that the kitchen was only now fit to eat it in. The voice chattered on. The man sounded more urbane than Paula's usual run of would-be escorts. 'I warn you, she won't be pleased to be pulled out of bed.' But, to Jo's surprise, Paula seemed, once she was fully awake, quite willing to get up and speak to her friend. Jo continued her breakfast preparations, making no attempt to be quiet. She wasn't going to creep around her own kitchen, just because Paula had declined to follow Marianne's example and pay for an extension in her room.

'Yes, Jo's still here. She's making toast.' Jo ignored the hint and listened unashamedly to Paula's half of the conversation.

'No, I missed it. Good job Briony didn't or we'd never've known.'

'Don't be silly. Of course it makes no difference, in

fact it adds a bit of spice. I don't promise not to giggle next time we . . . you know . . .'

'What, this morning? What time?'

'Well, I suppose so. I'm up now, aren't I?'

'Yes, of course I've told Marianne.'

'No, not her.' A covert glance at herself from Paula told Jo that the amusing snippet, whatever it might be, had not, and would not, come her way. 'But Marianne might have. Probably not, though. Marianne doesn't gossip.'

'No, that's too soon. Make it an hour. Byee.'

As Paula replaced the handset, Jo delivered her ultimatum, the reasons for it neatly tabulated. ' . . . So I'd like you out of here by the last of next month at the latest.'

Paula's reply was prophetic. 'Don't worry yourself. I wasn't going to be around for much longer anyway.'

Cavill Jackson never stood any nonsense from his brides. Twenty minutes before each one's appointed time of arrival he began his twenty-minute programme. He seldom played any very taxing items, since his purpose was merely to obliterate the unseemly twittering of females catching up on the family scandals since the last occasion – wedding, christening or funeral – that had given them sight of each other and the inside of a church.

If, by the final cadence, the current bride was not waiting in the porch, he would improvise for five minutes. He was not, after all, an unreasonable man.

After that, if she presumed to delay him further, he would embark on any piece that took his fancy. If she arrived just half a dozen bars into it, then she was the one who had to wait.

Today's bride had had her five minutes of his off-the-cuff variations on one of the wedding hymns and the congregation was getting audibly restive. He'd better begin on something loud. The D-minor toccata and fugue was somewhere under all this stuff on the stand. That should do nicely.

An expert flick and twist extricated the required sheets of music without dislodging anything else. Cavill flexed his fingers and hushed the whispering with Bach's first imperious call for attention before embarking on the elaborate trills and runs, intricately entwined.

When the echoes of the closing chords had bounced and jostled above the congregation's heads and died away, Cavill began to be seriously angry. His choirboys had more entertaining ways of spending their Saturday mornings than awaiting the pleasure of a spoiled daughter who was about to make some poor sucker a demanding wife. He twisted his mirror so as to see more of the nave. The groom looked more embarrassed than anxious. Cavill supposed there could be few predicaments more humiliating than being abandoned at the altar.

The one probationer choirboy tried to stifle a fit of giggles under the steely glare of his head chorister. Cavill sympathized with the probationer. He was prone to occasional fits of giggles himself. The conventional bit of *Lohengrin* was open in front of him. The silly girl had insisted on referring to it as 'Here Comes the Bride' when she was choosing her music. He stifled a wicked temptation to begin on it without waiting for her, and imagining the bewildered chaos that would ensue put him in a good mood again.

At last the light in the top left corner of the organ loft began to flash, the church warden's signal that the about-to-become Mrs Conway had deigned to put in an appearance. The vicar preceded the bridal party into the aisle. His dignified progress stilled the busy tongues until the bride and her entourage were clearly visible. Then further consternation was apparent. Something was obviously still not quite right.

The congregation consulted each other afresh, their vowels lost in the music but their sibilants cutting through it. However, the service proceeded without further delay.

'God our Father, you have taught us through your Son that love is the fulfilling of the law . . .' The beautiful voice was wasted on the language of the ASB, but the change from the 1662 Prayer Book had already been made when Tony was inducted at St Barnabas'.

When the first hymn was announced the congregation struck up strongly and cheerfully and Cavill forgave them their chattering. Now came the exchanging of the vows and rings. No more work for him till they all disappeared to sign the register. He listened idly. ' . . . That with delight and tenderness, they may know each other in love, and through the joy of their bodily union . . .' The young couple, who had been regarding the vicar solemnly, now exchanged secret smiles. Whatever had held the girl up, it was not a last-minute distrust of her man.

'It is given that they may have children and be blessed in caring for them . . .' What had been wrong, Cavill wondered, with the wonderful solemnity of having it 'ordained for procreation'? Tony had had the phrase, in any of its forms, omitted when, twelve months ago, at fifty-four years of age, he had astonished the parish by quietly marrying the housekeeper who had looked after him for almost a quarter of a century.

Cavill had seen their prim twin beds and suspected that the purpose of the vicar's nuptials had been the scotching of tentative but, in the nineties, unfortunately inevitable rumours about his sexual orientation.

Miss Johnson, having become Mrs Anthony Kirkbride, continued to produce gourmet fare and to hang spotless single sheets on the line in the vicarage garden. She had taken on nothing of the role of the traditional clergy wife, made no incursions into the MU or WI. The parish was happy, its population content to play peasants to Tony's squire.

Tony, in his vestments, looked like a bluff farmer in fancy dress and his working-class congregation loved him because of rather than in spite of his Harrow and Oxford education and private income. They treated the officers of the church rather as their medieval predecessors had done. When life got difficult, 'Mester Kirkbride' would see to it. His wife's effusive smile and anxiety to be of assistance made them feel hassled.

The present service was drawing to a close. The register was signed during yet another rendering of *Jesu Joy* by choirboys whose behaviour during the rest of the proceedings compared just a little unfavourably with that of the two small bridesmaids. Cavill's hands played the wedding march - Mendelssohn, what else? - leaving his mind free to observe that the groom's mother's wide-brimmed yellow hat rivalled the gold halo round the head of the angel in the west window.

He watched the boys file out of the choir stalls, more or less decorously, then let himself out of the organ loft, wondering if Jo would have given up waiting for him.

As he walked through his backyard and noted the back door left ajar to cool the kitchen, he saw that she had not. Jo stood at the cooker with her back to him, manifest only as a pair of long legs, a neat bottom and a curtain of hair shrouded in fragrant steam.

'It had better be a good story.' Her tone was preoccupied rather than aggressive. He relaxed and filled two glasses from the bottle of Côtes du Rhône that she had already opened. He was not sure when or where Jo had become an expert cook and he dared not ask. Whilst she busied herself with the final incantations of the magic spell that had turned his packet of supermarket sausages, a tin of chopped tomatoes and the tatty remnants of vegetation from his refrigerator's salad tray into haute cuisine, he began to set the table.

Their hands busy, they conversed easily and Cavill

described the morning's events that had delayed him. '... Tony told me after the service that the chief bridesmaid had failed to show, so I suppose it wasn't really the bride's fault. She couldn't decently slope off to church without allowing time for some minor accident to have delayed the girl. It's a good job I didn't follow the Bach with the Widor and make her wait through that, or the congregation would have died of starvation before they got to their wedding feast.'

'That organ loft's your little kingdom. You become a despot in it, and not a very benevolent one either!' Jo washed cooked rice with boiling water from the kettle and glared at him over it. 'So, what had happened to the girl?'

He shrugged. 'No idea. As far as I know, she's still missing. She's a student at a business college in Bradford, spending the weekend over here for the wedding. She went out with some boyfriend last night and never came back.'

Jo carried her spiced sausage casserole to the table. 'So, why did no one look for her last night?'

'The folk she was staying with lent her a key. They were a bit narked when she hadn't turned up by midnight, but they decided that she was of age and that they'd go to bed. When she wasn't there this morning, they assumed she'd spent the night either with the boyfriend or with the bride-to-be.'

Jo reached over and slapped Cavill's hand as it strayed towards the cruet. 'Don't smother it in salt and pepper before you've even tasted it! How come you know all this?'

Cavill's fork paused halfway to his mouth. 'Because Tony got in on the act as usual. The bridal party was anxious to get to the reception to welcome their guests, so he said he'd ring the girl's hosts again and, if they'd heard nothing, he'd advise them to inform the police.'

'And you hung around so as not to miss anything?'

'With one of your Saturday lunches in the oven? Not likely! But Mrs Parker was hanging around outside the vestry door and, when I spoke to her, she burst into floods of tears.'

'Was she one of the wedding guests?'

'No, she's Jon's mother.'

'Your delinquent whizz-kid? What's he done now?'

'He seems to have done a runner.'

'Well then, mystery solved. He's eloped with the chief bridesmaid. Find one and you'll find them both.' She glanced at him. 'Sorry, you're upset about the kid, aren't you?'

There was a lengthy silence during which each of them gave the food the concentrated attention it deserved. When their plates were empty, Jo reinforced her apology by scraping the remains of the casserole on to Cavill's and pushing the bottle towards him.

He accepted the food with enthusiasm but covered his glass. 'I'll recork it. I've saved this afternoon to practise the Lefebvre-Wely sorties. I've decided to finish my programme with them in Cologne next month. I'll have coffee instead.' To forestall a reiteration of her opinion that Jonathan was a waste of his time, he changed the subject. 'Did you see Tony's hour of glory last night?' She looked puzzled. 'Obviously you didn't. It was approximately three minutes of glory, actually.'

'What are you talking about?'

'He was interviewed on "Calendar".'

Jo was amused. 'I wouldn't have expected Tony to tout for custom that way.'

'Idiot, it was nothing to do with the church. There's an argument been going on locally for months.' He began to clear the table. Jo had been careful to specify that cooking meant just that. The washing-up was his responsibility. The gurgle of the coffee machine encouraged his efforts. 'They pulled down the old mill complex at Kingsbury last year, before it fell on somebody and cost the council millions in compensation. Tony's family owns the bit of land between the two buildings and rents out a row of garages on it. The Locost chain wanted to buy the land to build a supermarket on but Tony's holding out against selling his bit.'

'Is that chain spreading northwards, then?'

Cavill plunged greasy plates. 'Evidently. Anyway, through some legal technicality, there's a compulsory purchase order being served and the building plan's going ahead. The local shopkeepers are up in arms, of course.'

'They'll have a good spokesman in Tony. Did he demolish the opposition?'

Cavill came to sit at the table, leaving the clean dishes to drain. 'He was splendid at first. He made mincemeat of Locost's assurances that local trade would benefit from the crowds who'd be attracted to the new store. He waxed eloquent on the probable effects of increased traffic on local residents, had all the projected figures to hand, and explained why the council's plans for a new junction would be inadequate . . .'

'He would! So, what went wrong?'

'I'm not sure, exactly. I think he must have been under the impression that he was giving a radio interview. He suddenly seemed to become aware of the cameras, went to pieces and buzzed off.'

'Some people are like that with cameras. I don't much like being photographed myself.' She accepted the coffee cup he pushed towards her and he enquired after her household of student lodgers, wondering whether the coffee in her cup would dissolve the heap of sugar she had tipped into it. She stirred it thoughtfully. 'I have an idea they're up to something. I interrupted an obviously private conference in the kitchen last night. It involved much giggling and cramming into a briefcase whatever they'd been reading. They've probably reconvened now I'm out of the way. I'm going on to the library straight from here so they'll have all afternoon to get it out of their systems.' She drained her cup and refused a refill. 'Tempting, but I've three thousand words to finish by Monday. I'd better get stuck in or I won't be seeing you tonight.'

She pecked his cheek in passing, slammed the door of first the kitchen, then her Cavalier, and, reversing neatly on to the main road, disappeared into the distance.

*

Tony Kirkbride had been using an unusual lull in the weekend's demands on him to arrange his pulpit, ready for the next morning's service. Everything must be exactly where he expected to find it if his sermon were to be delivered with the usual illusion of spontaneity. Blu-Tack held his pages of notes down on the book-rest, lest a stray draught should deprive one of his anecdotes of its punchline. Everything was satisfactory now.

Standing in the shadow of the pillar against which the pulpit stood, Tony watched Cavill take his usual route to the organ loft, clambering over the decani stalls and scorning the neat door at the front end of the west aisle. He grinned as his organist kicked off his shoes and stowed them tidily on the lowest of the shelves beside him. Cavill's home bore witness to his congenital untidiness, but he had fished between the pedals for a tightly wedged shoe too often to risk it again.

His arrangements before he began to perform were as meticulous as Tony's own. He sat at the console exactly in the middle of the stool, adjusting its height so that his feet conveniently reached the pedals. He sorted his music into the order in which it would be required for Family Eucharist before covering it with a large-format manuscript.

His eyes on the staves, he rehearsed the piece mentally as he flexed his fingers and feet in preparation. Then, he began to play, though not, Tony thought, from the music in front of him. He thought he caught the echoes of a hymn tune and decided it must be an improvisation.

Whatever it was, it imposed an atmosphere of calm reverence, partly, he supposed, an effect of the resonance in the large building. Every sound lingered in the air and a series of rather louder chords seemed to float upwards before dying away, each one merging into the next to produce a continuous tone. It was as though someone had poured the sound in until the building was full.

Tony allowed himself a further thirty seconds to enjoy the effect before descending the pulpit steps and entering the chancel. His organist caught the movement in his mirror and swivelled round on his stool.

'Did your bridesmaid turn up?'

Tony shook his head. 'She wasn't waiting at the reception and she hadn't gone back to the place where she was staying. I advised the old couple there to report her missing. Did you sort out the tearful lady? Who was she? Thanks for coping with her, by the way.'

'Well, you already had your hands full. She's Beryl Parker.' Briefly, Cavill explained Mrs Parker's problem and his own connection with it through Jonathan's organ lessons. 'He scarpered on Wednesday and she's heard nothing since then. I gave her the same advice you gave the old couple – let the police know.'

Tony grinned. 'Perhaps they've eloped together. If they find one, they'll find both.'

Cavill smiled weakly and thought of Jon: quiet, shy-seeming, his hunched shoulders and caved-in chest hiding his real height. 'He doesn't strike me as the eloping sort.'

'How old is the lad?'

'Just twenty.'

'Old enough to take care of himself.'

Cavill sighed. 'Whether he can look after himself isn't the point. He's supposed to be on a course, a sort of alternative to a prison sentence. If he fails to keep the rules at this place it's tantamount to a breach of the probation order that sent him on the programme. That means going back to court, then it would be prison again.'

'A sort of vocational course?'

Cavill shook his head. 'The programme seems to be daily groups that discuss offending behaviour. They're made to face up to what they've done.'

'And he didn't fancy it and took off.'

'It's his mother he's taken off from. He likes the course – well, it's uncomfortable but he thinks it was helping him.' He glanced at his watch and excused himself from further conversation. ' . . . The programme for Cologne has to be finalized by the middle of the week and I shall be picking Jo up for tonight's concert at six-thirty.'

Tony too had duties which he enumerated. ' . . . And it's half past three now. Jean expected me half an hour ago.' He disappeared into the vicar's vestry and Cavill began to play the E-flat sortie. He loved its piquant harmonies, and the unexpectedness of its combinations, but today his mind was not fixed on them. When he had sensed Tony's movements behind him, he had hoped his silent audience would be Jonathan. Saturday afternoon was one of his regular practice times and Jon knew it. He played on for another half-hour but his musical disciple did not appear.

Marianne Baxter had risen late, completed with consummate ease the assignment her tutor had set, checked over a certain set of her rather complicated accounts and only then realized that it was well past lunchtime. She was extremely hungry. The previous day had been far too busy for the shopping to be fitted in but it would be all right to borrow something from the fridge and pay it back later. Jo knew she was meticulous about paying debts.

She could do with some company too. She was tired of her own. Jo was having lunch with Cavill but even Paula would do. She hadn't heard Paula blundering about or shouting this morning, but then, the girl had rolled home in the small hours. She might still be in bed.

She wasn't. Marianne, her head peering round Paula's door, wrinkled her nose at the sordid chaos revealed. She wondered how long it was since Paula had cleaned the room. Marianne could never have slept in it herself, cringed now even at the thought of having all this mess just on the other side of her wall. She was surprised that Jo tolerated it.

Marianne wandered downstairs and investigated the contents of the refrigerator. Paula must have had lunch out too. The Lean Cuisine calorie-counted meal she'd defrosted for today still sat on the top shelf. It would do. She would buy Paula another one when she did her shopping in the morning. She smiled at the large pink panel on the wrapper that laid out the contents of the packet, separated into fats, protein, carbohydrates and calories. If Paula drank less and stuffed less junk food, she'd keep in better shape at a considerably lower cost.

When the telephone rang, there was no one else in the kitchen to listen in to this second conversation held there by one of Miss Merry's paying guests. It was briefer than the earlier one. Marianne never wasted words.

'I could manage that, so long as the price is the same.'

'I didn't but Paula told me.'

'Shocked? Why should I be? It's your business.'

'I'll be there in about twenty minutes.'

She made no prophetic statement but her death was to follow as inevitably as Paula's had.

Chapter Four

After a chilly afternoon on the terraces of the local football ground, standing behind a young drug dealer who, on this occasion, innocently cheered his team to a one-nil victory, Detective Sergeant Benedict Mitchell was cold and disgruntled. Not able to take his eyes off his suspect to watch the game, he had actually come out of the ground ignorant of the score. Not that that concerned him – it was only soccer. Now, for once, he was pleased at the prospect of spending a brief period at a desk and close to a radiator writing up his report. In the station foyer, he stamped his feet and rubbed his hands, observed silently by Mark Powers, the laconic sergeant presently in charge of the desk.

His circulation restored, Mitchell strolled past the counter on his way upstairs. 'Anything interesting come in?'

Powers shrugged. 'Missing boy. CI's got his mother upstairs.'

'Oh yes? Better not interrupt 'em then.' Mitchell saw that Magic Powers was not amused. Fair enough. He wouldn't find it very funny himself if Declan got mislaid. 'How old?' Another shrug. 'Well, how long's he been gone?'

'Since Wednesday morning.'

Mitchell descended the few stairs he'd climbed. 'So why's she waited till Saturday afternoon?'

He expected to be answered with another shrug but Powers managed four more words. 'He's gone off before.' Appreciative of this unusual show of cooperation, Mitchell set off to report to his DCI, who also happened to be his father-in-law.

Browne seemed relieved to be able to pass the hysterical mother to Mitchell, offering him unwonted privileges as an apology. 'I've to see the Super, and it could be a long session. There's no point in disturbing Mrs Parker again. You can stay in my office. I'll get Karen to bring you some coffee. I'm sure Mrs Parker could do with another cup.'

Mitchell looked at the murky film over the untouched coffee in front of the sobbing woman and grinned at Browne, accepting the refreshments and the opportunity to occupy his superior's leather swivel chair as his bribe. He began his interview in his own inimitable style.

'Sergeant Powers tells me your son has run off before. You were so little worried about him that you've waited till he's been gone three days.' She hiccuped and raised watery eyes to his. 'In the circumstances, your present show of distress seems a bit excessive.' Good. She almost looked indignant. 'Perhaps you can pull yourself together whilst I read the CI's notes.'

As he absorbed the information already volunteered

by the bereft mother, Mitchell could hear that she was rooting in her handbag. When he looked up again, he saw that she had done as much as possible to restore her face to normal. It would be a conventionally attractive one, he allowed, once the red puffiness had disappeared. The youthful hairstyle did it no favours though. Two wings, of an assisted blonde hue, fell to chin level and emphasized the mature skin between them.

He considered needling her further but decided against it. 'If Jonathan's run off before and come back safe and sound, I take it he can look after himself. He isn't a child. Where did he go last time?'

She sniffed and mopped her face again with an inadequate, embroidered scrap of linen. 'He wouldn't give many details. He just said he'd stayed with friends.'

'Do you know who his friends are?' She shook her head. Mitchell tried to conceal his impatience. 'Have you got a good clear photograph of him, a recent one?'

She shook the wings of hair back. 'Are you trying to be funny? You've taken more pictures of him than I have.'

Light began to dawn on Mitchell. 'You're telling me he's been in trouble with us?'

'And then some!'

Mitchell waited, but, having admitted so much, she seemed reluctant to be specific. Mitchell smiled to himself, remembering the innumerable times in his childhood when he had been taken along to confession by his Irish mother. Putting his wrongdoings into categories and just admitting to a type of misdemeanour kept it all at a comfortable distance. He never minded, therefore, revealing his sins to Father O'Mahony. He'd already suffered worse at his mother's hands, literally as they were applied to the backs of his bare legs and mentally as she wormed out of him the mean and sordid little details of his actual crimes. He decided to let Mrs Parker off.

'All right, I can get the details from our records, and the photographs, though they aren't usually very typical. I could still do with a relaxed family one.'

'Family!' The tone was bitter. 'What family?' A tap on the door heralded Karen with the coffee. She placed it on the table and he waved her away, afraid that if his witness were interrupted she would not continue. Understanding the situation, Karen left without rancour. Easily the most abrasive of Cloughton's CID officers, Mitchell, surprisingly, seldom offended anyone. Recognizing the well of resentment contained in the woman opposite him, he poured coffee and pushed it towards her. 'Tell me about it.'

She drank most of the scalding liquid before remarking, 'What's sauce for the goose wasn't sauce for the gander.'

'Your husband played the field, then raised hell when you did the same?'

She nodded and bit her lip. Mitchell glowered at her so that she dared not begin weeping again. 'I lost count of his women. I only slipped up the once. When he found out he slammed out in a fury.'

'Don't you think you were well rid of him?'

'Jon and Steff didn't think so. Barry moved in with his woman of the moment and soon afterwards the kids moved in too. I was willing if that was what they really wanted.'

'And then?'

'Steff had enough nous to keep a low profile for a bit. Jon didn't. Barry threw him out and he came back, very unwillingly, to me. According to him, everything was my fault. Every time I did anything that didn't suit him, we had this caper.'

'He ran off?' She nodded. 'So, what set him off this time?' Mitchell immediately regretted the question as the floodgates opened once more. PC Caroline Webster, who had been silently scribbling her notes in the corner, produced a box of tissues, set it in front of Mrs Parker and immediately disappeared once more into the woodwork. Mitchell regarded Mrs Parker sternly. 'Don't start that again. It's not getting us anywhere. Go back to your story.' This time, the calculated aggression failed. The woman could not control herself sufficiently to answer him. Instead, she drew a largish envelope from her capacious handbag and pushed it towards him.

Mitchell took out a sheet of A4 paper. It was neatly headed with her son's name, but had then been turned sideways to accommodate a series of cartoon drawings. They featured two characters. A young girl was identified by a scribble of curls, a hair ribbon and a brief triangle of skirt above stick legs. A taller youth in the first picture was approaching a house. In the second, the girl was laughing at him, a large bubble attached to her head, filled with 'HA HA', much repeated and almost scoring the paper through.

In the third square, the girl was running away, obviously unsuccessfully, since, in the next, the boy held the girl by the hair. The fifth showed the figures seemingly floating in mid-air, the boy parallel to the girl and above her. The girl's bubble contained 'HELP'. The boy's was filled with question marks. The last picture showed the girl with taller figures ranged on either side. The boy stood alone, some distance away.

Mitchell studied the drawings for a long moment. 'This is what's upsetting you?' She nodded without looking up. 'Jonathan drew it?'

Now she looked up to defend him. 'I thought he did it to offend me but I was wrong.'

When he felt that his witness was cooperating with him, Mitchell could be as patient as the next man. Slowly he drew from her the story of her son's attack on the favoured sister, chosen to remain with the father, Jonathan's subsequent record of usually petty crime, the pleas Rory Jackson, his probation officer, had made on his behalf and the opportunity the courts had offered him to make good at Highfield House. 'What's all that got to do with the cartoon?'

'It was a piece of work he had to do. Rory will tell you all about it. And I didn't know, didn't stop to ask. I laid into him for nothing, just when he was doing so well. And he's always had a temper. He crashed off through the kitchen with no breakfast and no coat . . . Oh, he won't starve or freeze to death. His mates will give him anything he needs. And, in his present frame of mind, what they won't give him he'll probably steal for himself – money, radios, cameras, cars.'

Mitchell peered hopefully into the coffee pot but found it almost empty. 'What did you do after your son left on Wednesday morning?'

'I rang up Highfield House. When I said who I was they asked if Jon was ill, so I knew that he hadn't gone in. I said he had flu. As far as I know, that's what they still think.'

Mitchell had been sitting still for rather longer than he liked. Itching to be up and about the job, he hurried Mrs Parker through the rest of her story, extracting from her the telephone number of Rory Jackson and the name of his brother, Cavill. 'Your son wants to be an *organist?*'

'What's wrong with that?'

He watched her sweep out, glad he'd been able to provide her with a dignified exit line.

James Enright approached Jo Merry's house circumspectly. The row of substantial, late-Victorian semi-detached dwellings faced a tree-dotted grassed area that stretched as far as an equally substantial square-towered church of the same period fifty yards away. No two of the houses were alike. Jo's boasted a graceful white statue by a minute pool in the front garden and a narrow balcony with a stone balustrade round all of the first floor.

It must, James thought, have been left to her. There

was no way a postgraduate student could have afforded it, even if her grant were augmented by the proceeds from an occasional lecture or published paper. Since Ruth's rent was paid out of their joint account, he knew that Jo's lodgers were not subsidizing a mortgage to any great extent.

In James's pocket, as a feeble excuse for his presence if challenged, he carried Paula's latest essay – if essay was the right term for a collection of misspelled, ill-arranged random thoughts. No, Paula's efforts had produced little in the way of thoughts, even random ones. Meaningless phrases was a better description. Still, essay did mean try, and Paula had tried – her best and her tutors! – in the vain hope of obtaining a qualification that would lead to a lucrative life of ease.

Actually, Paula was naturally well qualified for just that. The object of James's visit was to remove evidence that he had enjoyed and paid for what Paula and her friends had to offer. He cursed the lascivious nature in which he had hitherto taken delight because evidence of that enjoyment might now prove a barrier to his marrying Ruth. He hoped he had judged his time of arrival accurately, early enough to have time to make a thorough search but late enough not to risk meeting Ruth before she left for her mother's house.

He wondered why she had chosen this particular weekend to visit her. She knew that this evening his orchestra was to give its most prestigious concert of the year. Not that Ruth would have appreciated it. Music was one more thing they did not have in common. Had they, in fact, anything in common?

He tried for the hundredth time to analyse the spell under which she held him. He would not have said they were suited at all. None of their colleagues or friends could understand them. He couldn't understand it himself. It was not a sexual attraction particularly, although that element in the relationship had been tested and not found wanting. He simply knew he had to have Ruth at least living with him, if not married to him, even if they never went to bed.

He wished that he had spent less of his previous social life in bed. It was not his conscience that troubled him. He had needs which had to be satisfied if he were not to be frustrated in his creative work, but he was unsure how Ruth would understand them. She realized he was not a virgin, of course. Neither was she but he suspected she had only enjoyed a physical relationship with men whom, at the time, she had believed she loved. She would be unable either to forgive or to understand his sleeping with women for whom he felt nothing, not even physical attraction, just because he enjoyed and needed sex.

As for actually paying for it, with a cut for everyone who helped to accommodate his requirements . . . James shook his head. It would be nice to be able to blot out the last five years. Still, all that was done with now.

He climbed the two steps leading to the front door and rang the imposing brass bell. He hoped his search wouldn't take too long. He had other essential tasks to get through and then he would have to make himself a meal and be ready, in the right frame of mind for his concert.

Since there was still no sign of his DCI with further instructions for him, Mitchell decided to escort Mrs Parker down to the foyer himself. With any luck, Magic Powers would offer him some other titbit that he could follow up, thus legitimately deferring his paperwork.

As he was seeing her safely into her sparkling Mini, he asked the questions he had been saving. Mrs Parker was not, he thought, a woman who would weep in a public place. 'Did the boy admit to assaulting his sister sexually?'

She shook her head. 'He denied it but the signs were there.'

'So why was he not charged with it?' He had misjudged her. Sighing, he provided a large handkerchief and waited. After a while, she looked up, sniffing. 'Was it because your daughter was known not to have been a virgin?' She nodded. 'Did you never get the whole story from him afterwards?'

She glared resentfully at him. 'Did your people get any more out of him?' Mitchell shrugged. 'Well, it's their job. If they can't sort him out, why expect it of me?'

Mitchell returned to the foyer and lingered, listening to Magic's side of a telephone call for long enough to understand that the report of a second missing person was coming in.

'Who now?'

Magic was succinct as always. 'A girl.'

Mitchell grinned. 'A boy and a girl? That simplifies things. They'll have eloped together. When we find one, we'll find 'em both!'

Summoned, as he had hoped, to help trace the missing girl, Mitchell was well pleased with life. He was surprised, when he arrived at Browne's office, to find no other officers were being briefed. Succinctly Browne shared the meagre information available. '. . . Her name's Briony Cocker. She's a student at some technical college in Bradford but she was spending the weekend in Cloughton with a couple called Staniforth because she was due to be chief bridesmaid at a friend's wedding this morning. We don't know yet where her permanent home is or who her family are. Mr Staniforth made the call to us after she'd missed the wedding. He didn't do it very willingly but the vicar and organist at the church insisted – somebody Kirkbride and Something Outlandish Jackson. They might have more to tell us later, but see the Staniforths first. The old man isn't too pleased with either of them or with us. Give them the works.'

Mitchell made for the door, pausing with his hand on the knob as the DCI's voice continued. 'By the way, I've read through the notes Caroline left me on Mrs Parker. You got a lot out of her – and as she looked quite composed as you brought her downstairs I gather that, by your standards, you were gentle with her.'

Where could the nosy sod have been, Mitchell

wondered. Instead, he asked, 'Would the Mr Jackson with the outlandish name be called Cavill?'

Browne's head jerked up. 'That's right. Know him?'

Mitchell shook his head. 'Sorry, but Mrs Parker told me that a Cavill Jackson was giving organ lessons to her son.'

'So, we have a connection.' Browne grinned. 'You never know, the missing couple might have gone off with one another. If we find one, we might find them both. Start looking in Gretna Green.' Mitchell forced his lips into a grin. Had Magic repeated his sally to Browne? And had it sounded so feeble first time round? He exonerated Magic. It would have to be a much more significant topic for him to waste so many words.

Caroline had little to say as they set off for Green Street, where Miss Cocker had been such a fleeting guest. Mitchell left her in peace and soon fell to meditating on a theme that was becoming an obsession. Would he ever catch up on the promotion plan he had drawn up for himself before he had met, courted, seduced and married Ginny? And then produced four kids, for God's sake! One of six himself, all reared in a four-roomed house with a bathroom extension taking up most of the space in a tiny backyard, he had vowed to produce a maximum of two. Or, in more optimistic mood, to have what his mother considered a good number and to make so much money that a nanny would keep them at the opposite end of his mansion until he had a fancy to play with them.

Still, each of them was a joy. Declan, tall, sturdy, serious, six years old and almost ready to join a team

– rugby, of course, what else? – well, cricket perhaps. Caitlin was an irresistible minx and they'd long since stopped regarding the addition of the twins as an unfortunate superfluity.

The Staniforths both came to the door to meet them. They were both so thin that, together, they failed to fill the doorway. The woman offered her hand. 'I'm Dora and this is Fred.'

Dora was flushed and animated. The disappearance of her guest was the most exciting thing to occur in her life for years. Fred seemed more worried. 'Will we be blamed?' he asked Mitchell, anxiously. 'She's over eighteen but she isn't twenty-one yet. Were we – well, *in loco parentis*, sort of?' For a moment, the satisfaction of having successfully brought off the Latin phrase distracted him.

'Being twenty-one doesn't signify any more. Being eighteen makes you legally responsible for yourself.'

The old man nodded his thanks to Caroline. It had obviously not been the girl's welfare that had troubled him.

His wife's excitement was increasing. 'She'd come over to be chief bridesmaid for our great-niece, Anna. You wouldn't miss something like that, would you, if it wasn't for a serious reason? I just know something's happened to her.'

Mitchell could imagine her disappointment if the girl turned up safe and sound. He asked the couple to give an account of the previous afternoon, beginning with the girl's arrival. They obliged, antiphonally.

'Well, she turned up in scruffy jeans with her hair all over the place.'

'Enjoyed her tea, though. Two lots of pie and two lots of crumble. Rather keep her for a week than a fortnight.'

'Did she tell you when she arrived,' Mitchell put in, 'that she'd be going out later?'

Both heads were shaken vigorously. 'I don't think she meant to then. She suddenly decided as we were sitting down, letting our tea digest. Mind you, hers'd be digested already, while I was doing the washing-up. She never offered to help.'

'She probably decided after sampling our company for an hour that we were too boring. Asked if we minded if she made a phone call.'

Mitchell waited for complaints about lack of payment but Dora admitted, grudgingly, 'Well, we didn't mind that and we did find the money on the telephone table when we were locking up at bedtime. I was just getting the photo albums out to show her Anna as a baby and she came back and said she'd been invited out for the evening. Did we mind if she had a key.'

'Well, we did mind, thought it was a cheek! But then Dora said she'd better have one if she was going to be late because we keep early hours. I wasn't too pleased but she'd said yes, so I just told her to come in quietly and have some consideration.'

'When she'd gone, Fred said he supposed we could trust a friend of Anna's, and she must be a good friend if she's her chief bridesmaid.'

A new thought occurred to Fred and his eyes gleamed angrily. 'Now she's made off with that key, we'll have to have all the locks changed.'

'She isn't a relation of yours, then?'

'Definitely not!' Dora obviously considered the question an insult. 'We were having this girl for the night as a favour to Anna's parents.'

'So, you didn't realize until you arrived at the church that Briony was missing?'

'Stupid fancy name!' Mitchell repeated his question. 'Well, there was a phone call this morning. Anna asked if she was on her way because everyone else had started getting ready. I told her we hadn't seen her since last night.' Mitchell blinked, attempting to sort out all the pronouns. 'Fine way to behave when she's supposed to be a guest.'

Mitchell was grateful for the glance from her husband that cut short this latest diatribe. 'How long have you been back home? I take it there's been no message since then.'

Fred shook his head. 'We came home soon after the meal was finished. Even watching all that energetic dancing made us feel tired . . .'

'Made us feel embarrassed, you mean. You should have seen them . . .'

Caroline's voice, coming from behind him, startled Mitchell. 'Did Briony have her wedding clothes here?'

'No. All the dresses were in Anna's bedroom.'

Caroline nodded. 'And did she go out in the clothes she arrived in?'

'Oh no. Scruffy jeans were good enough for us but the chap she was meeting was worth changing for. Not that she looked any better! The skirt she put on hardly covered anything.'

'Did she actually say it was a boyfriend she was meeting?'

Fred scratched his head. 'I don't think she did, but that was the impression we got. She was sort of excited, and . . . well, the clothes.'

Caroline seemed to have finished her contribution. Mitchell asked, 'I suppose you formed that impression partly from her side of the telephone conversation?'

Dora sniffed. 'It's out in the hall. Do you think we had our ears to the door?'

Mitchell thought exactly that. Fred grinned. 'We didn't but she made me turn the telly down right low.'

Dora's lips formed a tight line and Mitchell knew that this revelation would be paid for as soon as he departed.

It was half past six by the time Mitchell had written his reports and was ready to set off home. He would arrive by seven. He hoped the twins had kept to their schedule today. If they had, he would have the best part of three hours of Ginny's undivided attention before the ten o'clock feed. That would surely be long enough for what he had to say.

*

Though Edward had not wanted to kill Jo, he could see no way of avoiding it. Time was precious. He could not wait for her to go out again. Still, it was a pity. She had been very obliging when he rang, promising to put her car out on the road and leave the door raised so that he could drive straight into the garage. She'd be very surprised if she could see what his car was loaded with.

Now she was fussing with coffee cups in the kitchen. He had no time for all that. He passed through the door that connected the garage with the hall, fetching up outside the kitchen, and sniffed. On second thoughts, coffee would get Jo sitting down. He opened the sitting-room door for her and closed it whilst she was putting her tray on an occasional table. He took the chain from his pocket and slipped it quickly round her neck as she sat down, before she had a chance to pick up the jug and dispense its contents. He was obliged to strangle her but he was not vindictive. He had no desire to cause her the pain of scalding before she died.

When she had stopped first struggling, then breathing, he arranged her limbs comfortably, pulling her head back so that it rested on the cushion behind her. Then he walked round to the front of her chair to make the final adjustments. All his movements were neat, economical, efficient.

He was pleased now that he had allowed Jo to make the coffee. It would be a nice focal point for his photographs. After a few seconds' consideration, he went back to the kitchen for another two cups and saucers. The girls had better have one each. Yes, he liked the effect of a generous display of the expensive china. A few more deft moves and the table was arranged completely to his satisfaction.

Now it was time to bring the other girls in. He opened all the intervening doors before he began, to the hall, the garage and the boot of his estate car. He had no problem carrying the girls through. He had already dealt with the difficult part, breaking Briony's stiff joints to make them fit into the car, so that now she came out easily.

He placed Marianne and Paula at opposite ends of the huge couch and Briony had the remaining easy chair. Briony was difficult to arrange to his liking. She was stiff and awkward, however he placed the limbs, yet her neck had gone floppy again so that her head kept falling forward. He wouldn't put her in the foreground of any of the pictures after all. Glancing at his watch, he saw that he would have to be satisfied with the arrangement as it was. It would take a few minutes to get the settings right. That should never be rushed. If he made no mistakes with it, one roll of film should suffice. He took the pictures quickly and competently.

He thought that, when he had developed them, he would like the last shot best. This was the view from the doorway, the first view of the bodies the police would have when they were called. Jo and Marianne would be seen in profile, the best view of them both and it would hide Jo's messy nosebleed. It meant full-face views of Paula and Briony, but then, what would have made either of them look attractive?

Edward stowed away his equipment. He felt exhausted, but safe and comfortable again, ready to slip back into his everyday persona.

Chapter Five

If he had not been so miserably cold, Jon Parker would have been relatively content. The humiliation of crashing the Volvo was lost in his relief at being let off driving it, though he had not done it deliberately. It was a complete write-off, and it was amazing that he had not been hurt. At least Sola told him that he hadn't. Sola, though, hadn't got a wrenched neck and shoulder or a cut head.

Now he had produced a BMW from somewhere and Dez was to drive it. Jon half thought that Sola had given him a car he was afraid of just to humiliate him. He knew he had been the nearest the gang had to a leader before that spell in prison. Then Cracker, grown taller and bolder, had taken his place. He smiled bitterly to himself. Prison had knocked most of the stuffing out of him. Now Sola felt nothing but contempt for him, certainly no fear of rivalry. The big cars were probably nicked because a tinny little box on wheels would draw attention to itself in this well-heeled street.

Jon was now demoted to lookout. For reasons of his own, Sola had selected three posh houses in a well-to-do road in Kingsbury for their next job and Jon was ensconced in a convenient tree in the back garden of the middle one.

He didn't know what kind it was but it had a thick trunk and he had folded an old, dark-coloured sweater to make a comfortable seat where it divided into its two main branches. He was at just a convenient height to see up and down the back lane and down the wide shared drive of two of the houses that led to the front.

The tree had no leaves to hide him, but his legs were sunk into its ivy cladding and a tall, thick holly bush behind him screened him from passers-by in the lane. Not that there were many. The afternoon had been gloomy and bitter and Jon felt quite safe from discovery, though he seriously feared being frozen to death up here because his chilled limbs would refuse to carry him back to the ground.

He had had the three houses under observation, on and off, for two days now, long enough to be able to tell Sola how many people lived in 7, 8 and 9 respectively. The houses in this upmarket street were not numbered alternately since there was no facing row on the opposite side. Now his brief was to check who went in and out all day and to let Sola know immediately any of the three dwellings was empty.

Yesterday he had walked round them, carefully and discreetly, checking there were no boxes fixed to the outside walls advertising a burglar-alarm system. Any one of the houses might be protected by something cleverer, of course. This morning he had rung each one's telephone number, pretending to be a salesman of such devices. The woman at number 7 said they had made their own arrangements, thank you very much. A man at number 9 said he would give serious attention to some literature provided no one called. Number 8 had produced no response, though he'd rung so many times he'd lost count.

There had been nothing doing at number 8 all day. Jon was fairly sure the family was away, for which he was thankful. Its bedroom windows were the only place from which he could be seen if anyone looked hard enough. The folk at number 9 had been shopping this morning, come home and unloaded the goods, then watched television football until the curtains were drawn, and probably for a good while longer. The lights in the back room had gone out now and at least some of the family had left in a Granada.

He had the impression that number 7 was rented out in flats or rooms. The landlady wouldn't be popular. Splitting up these lovely houses and letting them out to people who came and went and had no pride of ownership was the kiss of death to these upper-crust districts. Yesterday and this morning, lots of girls had been coming and going. He had a feeling he had seen one of them before. This afternoon the coming and going had been mostly by men, including an aged poncer with a ponytail who had rolled up in an old Citroën estate.

That had been just before the woman had come back, and then Sola had walked up the drive and knocked on the door with his 'petition'. He didn't know whether the girl had signed it, but she had invited Sola in. He was sure to have found out what he wanted to know. He was good at it, being chatty, sounding interested. 'Have a nice day,' led to plans being exchanged and shared, and it was easy to ask who else lived there and when they'd be in because of getting more signatures.

Now a fourth visitor had come whom Jon definitely recognized, and he suddenly realized why the dark-haired girl had seemed familiar. She was Cavill's bird. He couldn't help to break into this house now – even if Sola tried to force him. Nevertheless, he sat, growing still colder, for another twenty minutes before yet another car drew up at the front, outside number 7 again, he thought. He heard the soft clunk of its door and a heavy tread. Peering through the dusk, he risked leaning forwards, away from the screening ivy.

Crikey! That massive copper, Green, was prowling round between 7 and 8. If one of the neighbours had spotted him in his tree and phoned the fuzz, he'd better scarper. Green had nicked him twice before already. When they needed to, Jon's limbs unexpectedly responded and he slid down the tree, wincing silently as his neck and shoulder muscles protested.

When he thought about it, PC Green held few fears for him. Since his mother didn't trust him he might as well go back inside and Green could do no worse than put him there. He shuddered to think, though, what Sola might do to a careless scout who'd put a job in jeopardy by being spotted.

*

Oblivious of Jon's scrutiny, Cavill Jackson had drawn up behind Jo Merry's car, then climbed out of and locked his own. Shivering, he saluted her ridiculous white statue that stood guard over the pool, its convex surfaces now reflecting orange light from the nearest sodium street lamp. He slipped round the side of the house, hammered on the back door, then let himself in without waiting for an answer.

He wiped his feet carefully on the mat, a habit enforced in this house though neglected in his own. He checked that the water in the kettle was covering the element and clicked the switch down, humming a few bars from the first movement of the Farewell Symphony, soon to be performed at the concert in which James Enright would play, and tickets for which were in his jacket pocket. Waiting for the water to boil, he passed through the hall towards the sitting room.

He stood for an immeasurable time in the doorway.

At some point he must, he supposed, have walked across to the piano behind the door. He found himself sitting on the stool, facing the instrument, his back to the ghastly figures that surrounded the coffee tray. He reached for his mobile phone from the pocket inside his jacket and punched three nines. His lips were stiff as he asked for the police and briefly described the scene in the room. He agreed to a request to remain on the premises and to touch nothing.

He reneged on his promise to the extent of fingering the piano keys. His hands had moved without his volition and he became aware that they were playing a Schubert impromptu, the C-minor, plaintive and appropriate. Had he played the dramatic opening bars? He couldn't remember. He finished the piece and let his hands rest on his knees. Jo liked Schubert but this wasn't her favourite impromptu. She preferred the A-flat major. Suddenly, it became of overriding importance to play it for her one last time.

Mitchell had hardly begun on the hard word he had determined to give his wife when a thin wail interrupted him. For once, Virginia ignored it. Even when the second infant, roused from slumber by the unattended first, joined in his complaint, she kept her attention on her husband's face and words.

She had the impression that he had been rehearsing the latter. Benny seldom delivered his thoughts in this neatly tabulated form. ' . . . I think I've paid my debt and more. I can still see your point of view. You had to finish your degree, and, by the time you'd got it, you were tied to the house with a small boy and a baby. It was a good idea to carry on studying and keep your brain sharp. I was proud when you got your MA, proud of *us*, of doing my bit with the house and the kids as well as of your achievement.' Virginia bit her lip, knowing it would be fatal to smile at his agitated pacing.

'But enough's enough. I'm thirty-three and a sergeant, only one rung up the ladder and that only by default. It's my turn. If you want to use the qualifications you've earned, get a job, that's fine, but it'll be up to you now to make the domestic arrangements.'

'With twice as many kids?'

Benny looked yet more uncomfortable, and the cries of the five-week-old babies redoubled. 'That's only half down to me.'

'OK.'

'OK what?'

'OK, I'll take responsibility at home until you've got your inspector's exams, whether or not I can fit in a job.'

'You don't mind?'

'I was beginning to think you were never going to get on with your own career. I was grateful for all your support at first, but I've been starting to wonder whether I was becoming a convenient excuse. I minded that. I go along with everything you've said – except one.'

The shrill peal of the telephone added itself to the background cacophony and prevented Mitchell from enquiring about his wife's one reservation. He grimaced and reached for the receiver, listened, whistled and scribbled down directions. 'I'll be there in ten minutes. Is Dr Stocks there? What about Ledgard?'

'A body?'

'Not one but four!' He tried to look shocked and grieved to mask his already burgeoning excitement. 'Look, Ginny, obviously I've got to go, but we must talk about this soon.'

Virginia wrinkled her nose at him, on her way to attend to their screaming offspring. 'We already have. Get studying – when you've sorted this lot out!'

*

Mitchell departed feeling pleased with life. He could never work out whether things usually turned out to suit him or whether he was adept at making the best of things however they turned out. He had thought he wanted a clear evening of domestic bartering, hammering out terms. He should have known that he and Ginny could settle things in a few sentences - not because they always agreed but because Ginny always said what she meant, never played games with him like most females did, and that kept things uncomplicated.

She was soon going to be put to the test. Four bodies should keep him fairly short of time in the near future, and he was still determined to make a prompt start to his studies. It was no good waiting for favourable circumstances. They never happened.

His thoughts returned to the reason for his journey and he wondered if the number of bodies would have increased before he arrived. A mass killer often continued on his spree until he finally turned his weapon on himself. He hoped this one would do neither, mostly for the sake of potential victims, but also, he had to admit, because there might be much to clear up in that sort of incident but not a great deal to investigate.

A reprehensible anticipation, definitely pleasurable, kept Mitchell's foot down hard on the accelerator on his way to Kingsbury, the ex-village that attached Cloughton to Bradford. Number 7 Kingsgate he saw was marked by a police car outside in the drive and a ridiculous statue in the garden. Mitchell blessed its location. Another couple of streets north-east and this quadruple-murder investigation would have been Bradford's pigeon. A mile further south and he would have had, coming as he was straight from home, little chance of being first on the scene – except of course for the constable whose beat this was. As he climbed out of his own vehicle, he willed the beat bobby to be green and raw so that he would have done little but stand guard. A mountain of muscle topped by a helmet appeared at the front door and introduced himself. Whatever he was by nature, the constable was certainly Green by name.

As he followed him into the house, Mitchell heard music coming through an open door, lively trills and crashing chords on a piano. He spoke to the constable's back. 'Someone left a CD on?'

Green replied over his shoulder. 'No, he's playing the thing himself.'

'Who is?'

'Red-haired chap. I spoke to him but he took no notice. He wasn't doing any harm so I left him to get on with it.' Mitchell gave the PC an old-fashioned look. He responded indignantly. 'I'd have gone back in sharpish if the music had stopped.'

Mitchell shrugged. 'I suppose, if he wanted to hide anything, he's already had all the time he wants. I take it he is the one who called us?' He walked into the elegant sitting room and regarded first the four figures at their ghastly coffee party and then the pianist's back.

Mitchell was not musical but he thought the man was playing well. He didn't seem the arty type. Looked more like an athlete, slight but muscular with close-cropped hair. He was not dressed for athletics, but wore a formal suit. Mitchell tapped him on the shoulder. The man swivelled on the stool and blinked at the two officers as though he was surprised to see them.

'Thought they'd appreciate a little concert, did you?' Leading Jackson away from the grisly scene to a convenient group of chairs in the entrance hall, Mitchell nodded to Green to take notes. Jackson sank on to the chair Mitchell indicated and regarded him uncertainly.

'Cool customer, aren't you?' Jackson made no response. 'When we asked you to remain on the premises, we hardly expected you to keep the corpses company.'

'That's where the piano was.' Mitchell waited but Jackson evidently considered that the implied question had been dealt with.

'Did you think one of them was going to vandalize it? Tow it away?'

Jackson regarded Mitchell wearily for some moments, then said, with no affectation, 'When I meet a crisis, I escape into music. When I walked into the drawing room, I was as shocked as you would expect. It wasn't a conscious decision. I don't remember walking to the piano, I just found myself playing. I'm still on automatic pilot now. I haven't faced what's happened yet.'

Mitchell soon regretted his aggressive opening. Cavill Jackson was subdued but cooperative and Mitchell, who seldom needed to go back on his first impressions, liked him. The man's general demeanour was youthful but slightly veined hands and fine lines about the eyes suggested mid- to late thirties. The teeth were good and the red hair thick, probably cut so short because, like his own, it refused to be disciplined.

Jackson looked shaken and upset but he had himself well in hand, considering he had just stumbled upon not one but four bodies, one of them that of the girlfriend he had been about to escort to a concert. Maybe giving a piano recital was how a musician reacted to finding a roomful of corpses.

Mitchell considered passing his witness on to Green and spending the time until Browne arrived in a scrutiny of the scene and the victims. He decided against it. He'd keep the man talking and see what slipped out. Seeing that Jackson had turned away from him, he asked hurriedly, 'Were you and Miss Merry engaged?'

Cavill shook his head slowly, as though he were having difficulty making up his mind.

'You hoped to be, maybe?'

'It was Jo who hoped.' Cavill turned back politely to his interrogator. 'Everyone accepted us as a couple. I was happy with that but . . . Well, it sounds self-indulgent but I'm too committed to my career to want or be able to be permanently committed to a person. It sounds as if I was just using her. Maybe I was. Tony thought we should live together for a while, see how things worked out.'

'Tony?'

'Vicar of St Barnabas'. I'm his organist. He's my mentor, sort of substitute father.'

'Funny sort of suggestion to be coming from a vicar.'

Cavill smiled. 'He lives in the real world. Working on the Highfields Estate, you don't have much choice about that. I don't think it would have worked, living together. Jo had her own talents and ambitions. I wouldn't have wanted her to give them up . . .' His voice trailed away as they heard the front door open.

Mitchell's feelings were mixed as his DCI came in and dispatched Jackson to Green's keeping to await their further attentions. He might not be so chatty when they questioned him again. Still, Browne's priorities had to be accepted now he had arrived.

Mitchell liked his father-in-law and was glad to work under him. Mostly he was allowed to do things his own way and he suffered reasonably cheerfully for the mistakes he sometimes made. The most serious had been seducing Browne's daughter. Marrying her, though, had brought him the very opposite of the conventional benefits. Browne had to be seen to be offering him no favours, for both their sakes. For this to be generally acknowledged by their fellow officers, the DCI had sometimes actually to discriminate against him.

Mitchell's ebullient nature protected him, together with Virginia's rather offbeat but unfailing support. At least, having been brought up as a policeman's daughter, she never complained about the lonely and unpredictable lot of a policeman's wife.

Mitchell allowed Browne a short space to take in

the bizarre scene. The sitting room, Edwardian in its proportions, had a wall of well-filled bookshelves and another taken up with a huge bay window. On the two longer walls, a restrained paper in silver on duller grey emphasized, together with grey rugs on parquet, the gleaming white of the woodwork. The whole was warmed by the dusky rose of soft furnishings. A Royal Albert coffee set was resplendent on a low table big enough to hold it all safely.

In the midst of this elegant splendour sat the lifeless quartet. Maybe Briony and Paula, even animated, would have seemed out of place. Apart from the clash of the fuchsia pink of Paula's jacket with the chair cover behind her, which was just unfortunate, these two didn't fit. Tarty, Mitchell decided, though he could see that their vulgarity of attire was not an inexpensive one. As she was responsible for the decor, Jo should have appeared an appropriate doyenne. It was all the more shocking, therefore, that the lower part of her face and the front of her clothes had been stained and dirtied by blood from her nose, which was still moist, though no longer flowing.

Mitchell, armed with the information he had received from Cavill Jackson, identified the girls for Browne, rather like a helpful host at a party, at least until he came to the less attractive ones. 'This is Jo Merry, the one Mr Jackson came to collect. She's a postgrad student at Bradford. Did her first degree at Oxford. The house is hers and two of the others are her student lodgers. The one in black and white is

Marianne Baxter. Jackson says he's never seen her dressed in any other colours.'

Mitchell thought this girl had sounded the most interesting of the trio Jackson had described, and they regarded her in silence for a moment. She was clad in black leggings and a close-fitting black sweater. Black leather boots were laced up almost to her knees and a white shirt was knotted carelessly across her flattish chest. Her mousy fair hair was baby-fine and fell from a centre parting to chin level. On her right it was neatly tucked behind her ear. On the left fine strands spread over her face. She wore no make-up except for black lines around the eyes.

'That type aren't usually the demure little misses they look.' Having passed judgement on Miss Baxter, Mitchell wandered back to Jo Merry. She too was dressed in black and white. Her checked skirt was winter-weight but short, revealing legs worthy of the sacrifice of a warm covering. A matching jacket was tossed on a small armchair across the room. 'Very elegant,' Mitchell gestured at the garments, 'but too thick and warm to be worn in a concert hall unless the heating had broken down. She must have been killed before she got ready for the concert, but not too long before. She's still quite warm.'

Browne was studying Jo Merry's face. 'Reminds me of Sophia Loren. The features are rather Italianate, a bit coarse but probably very alluring when she was smiling and animated.'

Mitchell sniffed. 'She hasn't got a right lot to smile about at the moment.' He passed on. 'The fat, painted one is Paula Carey.' He pointed to the figure that shared the sofa with Marianne, exotically colourful in contrast with her companions' neutral tones. Her ample breasts were lent added bulk by a fluffy knitted jacket. Her face was encrusted with a pseudo-tan and the singing pink of the jacket was reproduced on her lips. Not much to recommend her, Mitchell decided, though the hair was good: long, thick and curly, with a hint of chestnut lighting up the brown. The mottling of the skin with petechiae was absent from this girl's face and neck.

'This one,' he observed to Browne, 'probably died of shock before the ligature did its job. Seems to have been some kind of chain. She's a mess, isn't she?'

Browne raised an eyebrow. 'Do you always write off women you don't find physically attractive?'

Mitchell shook his head amicably. 'No, only the fat ones.'

'They can't help it . . .'

'Of course they can. That's the whole point! It means they're sloppy. They haven't the self-respect to improve what they can.'

Browne took a long hard look at Mitchell's considerable though muscular person, then let him off. 'And this last girl?'

'I don't know. Jackson has never seen her before.'

'So, she doesn't live here?'

'No, but another girl does. Ruth Roberts. She's away visiting her parents till tomorrow. I wonder if the killer thought this other girl was the fourth resident?' Browne nodded slowly as Mitchell hurried on. 'It's not the usual sort of mass killing. And they weren't all killed here. The last three would hardly have queued up for their turn. Even if they'd been locked in, presumably they'd have fought or tried to escape.'

Browne nodded again and turned to the window. 'Where the hell are Stocks and Ledgard? We can't go far on this one without the medics and the lab.' As though he had produced them by wishful thinking, the two doctors appeared from opposite directions almost simultaneously and parked outside the house next door, the space immediately in front of number 7 being occupied by its late owner's Cavalier and Cavill's Maestro.

Mitchell joined Browne at the window and watched Dr Stocks sprint up the drive. 'He's getting in first before Ledgard makes him redundant. He is anyway. We don't need his bit of paper to tell us these people are dead!' Mitchell was not particularly disappointed to be dismissed from the conference between the DCI and the two doctors. Stocks would be off almost as soon as he'd arrived and Ledgard would give little away until he had checked and rechecked his conclusions in his lab. Anything he did offer Browne would scrupulously share with his team.

What team? Mitchell asked himself as he rejoined Green in the spacious hall. The men with whom he had served his early days as a CID officer had peeled off one by one, succumbing to the claims of young children, promotion to other forces, ill health and better chances of promotion in the uniformed branch. He could not think of another CID officer in the station who was not already busy on one of the many and various investigations currently being pursued on their patch. Mitchell liked to work under pressure but even he quailed at the idea of just himself and the DCI following up four killings.

He was slightly cheered by the arrival of two more vehicles bringing seven more uniformed officers. When Browne ignored the noise of their arrival and remained closeted with Dr Ledgard, Mitchell deployed two of them to cordon off the house, garden and part of the street. 'The rest of you had better go on the knocker, you as well, Green. You must be cheesed off with hanging around this hall. I've got to so I'll stay here for now.'

Having secured for himself an excuse to be on the spot for whatever might happen, Mitchell switched on the kettle to reheat the water Cavill Jackson had already boiled and left his mind blank to see which questions floated to the surface. Could the ferret-faced fourth girl be the missing bridesmaid? If so, what connection was there between her and the others? Were the girls killed because they were here and saw something that someone wanted to keep secret – or were they killed because, as a household, they had made someone angry? If so again, was Ruth Roberts in danger? And what, if anything, did the missing boy, Jon Parker, have to do with it all?

The kettle clicked off and Mitchell heard the expected sounds of Dr Stocks's departure. He made coffee for himself and Jackson. Until Browne appeared, the most useful thing he could do was to persuade this mad musician to tell him more.

He carried the coffee mugs out into the hall and joined Jackson on a chair just inside the door. He had learned a great deal from his DCI in the last seven or eight years, not least of which was the value of the oblique approach on certain occasions, not one that came naturally to him. He'd do his best. 'I suppose missing your concert is the least of your worries at the moment. Still, it was a pity. What were you going to hear?'

Jackson looked first surprised at the question, then marginally animated. 'One of the Leonora overtures and then Haydn's Farewell Symphony in the first half. The second half was to be a surprise. James wouldn't tell us.'

'James?'

'Dr Enright. He plays in the university orchestra.'

'Bradford?'

Jackson nodded. 'He's Ruth's boyfriend and he made us all buy tickets. Paula and Marianne were two of his students.'

'Subject?'

'English. That's what Marianne was reading. Paula was supposed to be doing business studies and that included one lecture and one tutorial a week from James.'

Mitchell raised an eyebrow. 'Supposed to be doing business studies?'

Jackson almost managed a grin. 'Don't ask James that. It'd be the last question you managed to slip in before he gave you a peroration on the quality or lack of it in today's students, how they're really dole customers pushed into further education to make government statistics look better. He says he's had to abandon nearly all his traditional courses in favour of providing entertainment for morons.'

'Was Paula a moron – in your opinion?'

Jackson shrugged and looked rueful. 'Yes. I suppose James has a point but he goes to the other extreme, wants to live in an ivory tower. I try not to myself, though it's a temptation sometimes, up in an organ loft, in charge of all that noise and power. I could make a living just doing recitals like the one I'm giving in Cologne in three weeks' time. Or I could take a cathedral post. I've been offered several, but I like to live among ordinary people. I like the challenge of an ordinary parish church where my choristers have no musical tradition or background and have to be taught everything.'

Mitchell wondered whether his colleagues would be allowing Jackson to fly off to Germany if the case had not broken when the time came. He debated whether to let his witness ramble on, in his attempt to dissociate himself from the horror next door, or whether to divert him to the subject of his girlfriend. Deciding it was time they got down to business, he still avoided a direct approach to that particular subject.

'Very soon, we'll have to get on to one of the force's least pleasant duties, giving bad news to the victims' next of kin. Would you be able to help us with any names and addresses?'

Jackson shrugged. 'I expect it's parents for Marianne and Paula. Ruth will probably have the details, and James will give you her own parents' telephone number if you want to speak to her before she's due back tomorrow. Jo had no one. She was illegitimate. Her mother neglected her and didn't keep in touch when she was taken into care . . .' He paused, looking uncomfortable. 'She'd have moved heaven and earth to stop you knowing about that if she were alive.'

Mitchell was puzzled. 'You said she was still studying?' Jackson nodded. 'So where did all this come from?' Mitchell's gesture took in the size of the establishment and the quality of its furnishings.

Jackson looked anxious and answered still more reluctantly. 'I fear she was overcharging the girls to pay her mortgage . . .'

The sitting-room door opened and for a second time Browne interrupted Mitchell's conversation with this young man, just as it seemed likely to reveal useful insights into the nature and relationships of the victims. Ledgard, still fastening his case, followed Browne out and made for the door. Before the two officers could confer, a stentorian voice demanding a more convenient parking place heralded the arrival of Superintendent Petty. Mitchell scowled. 'That knocks any more progress on the head for a while.'

Browne's lips thinned but he merely remarked, 'He's bringing reinforcements, a Holmes-trained sergeant on the loose after covering a maternity leave in Manchester and a couple of DCs with a promise of more to follow.' He glanced across at Cavill, who was draining his coffee cup, and raised his voice. 'I think we can let you go home for the moment, Mr Jackson. You'll have to come in to the station at some convenient time to sign your preliminary statement when Sergeant Mitchell has it ready, though, and I'm sure we'll need to speak to you again. Constable Green will drive you.'

'But I've got my own . . .' Mitchell watched it dawn on Jackson that his car was to be examined by the forensic team, and that he was being seriously considered as a possible killer of the four young women. He looked shocked rather than angry. Mitchell felt indignant on his behalf. It occurred to him that this was the second time he had had to investigate a suspect who had an obsession with music. He had liked the other one too.

On his way out, Jackson let in the new contingent of officers. Mitchell slid into the kitchen in an attempt to avoid a confrontation with the Superintendent. The strange but likeable Jackson had given him much food for thought, but he was wondering whether he had overdone his proudly acquired oblique approach. He might find himself off the case if he had not elicited enough hard facts to fill out into the kind of preliminary statement Browne would expect to appear in the case file.

Chapter Six

Babasola Ogunade rolled over between his black and white sheets and looked down on the girl whose blonde hair streamed across his black and white pillow. English roses weren't his usual type but she'd been good. He examined in detail such parts of her as the duvet revealed.

She bore almost no physical resemblance to her brother. She was quite attractive in her own way. He'd better make the most of her. She might not be so cooperative after he'd shopped the young halfwit. He'd expected incompetence. After all, the idiot had been nicked times without number and had already done a stretch. He'd only allowed him to join them to humour Cracker. Now he was wanting to waste three days' preparation and scrub a job because one of the designated houses belonged to a friend of a friend. Time for him to go home to Mummy.

It was a pity he hadn't written himself off along with the Volvo. It would have given Sola a great deal of pleasure to see the lad off personally, but why risk trouble for himself when the police would take him off their hands? He could set him up tomorrow, have him in custody by bedtime. No reason really for Steff to know anything about it.

He slid out of bed and was halfway into his trousers when he noticed her watching him, a silly half-smile on her face. God! She wasn't going to be one of those clingy, adoring ones, was she? Better snap her out of it.

He turned his back on her before he spoke. 'Come on, get up! What are you waiting for? You're not expecting me to pay you, are you?' If she cried, she'd be out. He waited.

She didn't. He even saw a flicker of spite in her eyes.

'I'll have to think about what to charge. Did you pay Briony?'

'Pay ferret-face? She ought to have paid me!' Fool! A bit late now to ask who on earth Briony was.

Stephanie propped herself up on her pillow and began to enjoy herself. 'She's after more than a one-off payment, you know. She's three months on. Not that you satisfied her. There are plenty of others it could have been but she's got to pick on you in case it's black. You could have given her a white baby but none of her sugar daddies is likely to be the father of a black one.'

His dressing complete, Sola had been admiring his handsome features in the dressing-table mirror. Now he wheeled round, fists clenched. 'I'll shut her mouth for her, and you'd better watch out that I don't shut yours.'

*

The sound of the door latch closing told Mitchell that his DCI and Superintendent Petty were back in the murder room. It was safe to come back to the hall and survey the extra men the Super had brought with him. He knew the two DCs by sight. Winters looked up from the pocketbook in which he had been scribbling notes, winked and jerked his head in the direction of the other two figures by the front door.

DC Craig was parading his charms to a girl who stood with her back to Mitchell. So, Manchester's spare DS was female. Life was looking up. She was slight, perhaps thin, a shade over middle height with a neat cap of cropped dark hair. She was dressed for action in a pair of smart, pressed jeans, highly polished flat shoes and a sheepskin jacket flung over one shoulder. Something in her stance stirred a memory. Mitchell was pleased to see that she seemed unimpressed by Craig's macho posturing.

He walked towards her. 'If you're the relief sergeant, shall we introduce ourselves?'

She swivelled on one heel and eyed him warily. 'Hello, Benny.'

Mitchell stared for five full seconds before his face broke into a delighted grin. 'Jennie!'

She didn't return the smile, merely corrected him reprovingly. 'Jenni*fer*.'

Mitchell blinked. 'Jennifer. Right. Only, don't try Benedict on me.'

The two DCs, sensing tension between the two sergeants, backed away, leaving them to work it out. Once armed with the coffee that seemed to be on general offer, however, they stood in the kitchen doorway, enjoying Mitchell's discomfiture. It was not his normal condition.

Mitchell wondered how to go on. It seemed unhelpful to say he was still having difficulty even recognizing the woman who, until a couple of years ago, had been a respected colleague and a good friend. He and Virginia had agonized over the short letter of commiseration they had sent when Jennie's husband had been killed a short time after her family had left Cloughton. Had it offended in some way?

They had written again when her second daughter had been born, three months later. This letter and their small gift had been acknowledged briefly but graciously. To gain time, he offered her coffee, which she refused, and the scant information so far accumulated on the case. She had done her homework promptly. Only the details he had obtained from Cavill Jackson were new to her.

Whilst he was casting around for a way of enquiring after her remaining family that would not incur another snub, Browne and Petty came out of the sitting room. The DCI escorted his superintendent out to his car, then returned, tight-lipped, to glare into the kitchen at the remains of the coffee party.

Icily, he addressed Mitchell. 'Did the SOCO boys come and go whilst the Superintendent and I were conferring? How much have you disturbed? What the hell's wrong with you today?'

Mitchell opened his mouth and shut it again. Browne's temper was not likely to be sweetened by his intended reply. After inflicting several seconds of silent displeasure, Browne turned to his adopted sergeant. 'Glad to have you back with us, Jennie.' Mitchell waited to see whether the DCI too would be put in his place, but she gave him a cool nod and thanked him.

The sight of the scene-of-crime team's car pulling into the drive to replace the Superintendent's Mercedes seemed to mollify Browne. Dispatching Craig and Winters to join the house-to-house enquiries, and leaving the men who had cordoned off the murder scene to guard it, he beamed at the photographer who was manoeuvring an armful of cumbersome equipment through the door.

'We'll get out from under your feet,' he promised. 'If there's anything urgent you need to tell us tonight, ring the Fleece.' He nodded to his two sergeants. 'Only one, mind.' Mitchell nodded happily. At least he was not in sufficient disfavour to be left out of the invitation.

Cavill Jackson stood in the vicarage garden for almost a minute before finally making up his mind to mount the two steps to the front door and ring the bell. The day seemed to have lasted half a lifetime, but it was only a quarter past nine. A crack of light appeared at the end of the hall, broadened as a door opened wider, then was obliterated as a figure came through.

Cavill's spirits plummeted. That was the kitchen and this was Jean. He didn't think he could stomach her well-meant sympathy. He wished he had gone straight home. Perhaps she did too. Her automatic flashlight smile was shot through with something other than pleasure at seeing him – disapproval? Anxiety? Perhaps it was just surprise. Saturday evening was not his usual time to call.

He wondered how to tell her that her coffee was excellent but he couldn't swallow it, and knew there was no way he could bring himself to explain to her why he had decided to come. It didn't matter. Even if he had been able to find the words, he wouldn't have had the mental strength to interrupt her own compulsive flow.

'Tony's hardly been in for a minute, ever since Friday lunchtime. He's been keeping an eye on the Betts family whilst Denis is in hospital – and visiting him there of course, plus covering a lot of the things in church that would normally fall to Denis – and then there's been old Mr Oliver. I tried to tell him Walter Oliver's a naughty old man who plays games with everybody, but he just said it wasn't like me to be uncharitable – so he's having to finalize the arrangements for the Sunday services now. I don't really want to interrupt him . . .'

Cavill tried to still the quivering of his fingers round his coffee cup whilst Jean fussed around the kitchen. He tried to make his mind a blank. Failing, he attempted to concentrate on Jean's face, ignoring the babble of words issuing from her mouth. It was red and weather-beaten and her eyebrows and lashes seemed to have been worn away. She had teeth like a horse, big and square, with the roots showing when she gave her terrifying smile. Her chin was a bump below her bottom lip that bobbed about on the land-slide of jaw that became neck and disintegrated into breasts that jostled one another as she bustled about.

His mind surfaced again and he tried to listen to what she was saying. '. . . You'll have to excuse me babbling on. I always get like this when Diana and Mrs K. are coming. Tony likes to have them often. He and Diana are very close, considering the age difference. They've always kept in touch. Even when Tony had a living in Truro, just after my parents died, she'd come down from Yorkshire at least every couple of months. She'd stay a week or so then, to make all the travelling worthwhile. Mrs K. came as well, of course . . .'

Having disciplined his hands, Cavill sipped from his cup and was surprised to find the coffee beneficial. He drank deeper. '. . . They never bothered me in those days. It was Tony's house and I was under his orders – not that he ever did order me. Now it's my own household it's different. They don't dislike me exactly, but Mrs K. hoped Tony would marry a young girl. She has this obsession with keeping everything in the family. I don't know who she'll leave it all to now. I'm well past all that, and it doesn't look as if Diana's going to oblige. Even if she did, it wouldn't suit madam because the name would be different.'

Cavill drained his cup and Jean refilled it without consulting him. 'I can't think what to wear tomorrow. Not that Diana won't outshine me, however much trouble I take.'

The kitchen door opened and Tony's head appeared. He grinned at his wife and got out a cup for himself. 'I thought I could smell coffee.'

Jean peered into the pot and nodded, satisfied that it would provide for her husband. She handed him his cup. 'I'm glad you finished earlier than you expected . . .'

As she poured, he had been examining his organist's face with some concern. 'I haven't, I'm afraid. I'm delighted to see Cavill. For his company, of course, but I'm hoping he'll bear with a couple of last-minute changes to Family Eucharist and now I don't have to ring him. And you'll face tomorrow better if you get an early night.' Jean could take a hint if it was broad enough and, after tidying the tray, she obediently left them.

'The study, I think.' Tony gathered up both their cups and shepherded Cavill up the hall and into his office. 'Did you come to talk about it?'

'The Eucharist?'

'About whatever's wrong.'

'How did you know . . .?'

'You don't usually honour us on Saturday nights and you never come looking like this. Is it Jo? Have you split up?' The silence lengthened. 'I'm sorry. Have a whisky and I'll shut up.'

'No. Yes . . .' Cavill wiped his face wearily with his hand. 'I do want the whisky and I do want to talk to you, but now I'm here I don't know where to begin – and Jean . . .'

Tony smiled. 'She can't help it, you know. She so

much wants to help everyone but she hasn't the sensitivity to know where not to tread, and her huge inferiority complex gets in the way too. Sometimes I wish I hadn't married her. Oh, I'm just as fond of her as I ever was, but she was happy and relaxed when she was working for me. Somehow, making her my wife has created problems for her that I should have foreseen. It's funny how you can find very sensible advice for everyone but yourself.'

He handed Cavill a good inch of Glenmorangie in a Waterford tumbler. 'Tell me the worst bit and then the rest of it will be easy.'

He listened in silence from Cavill's shaky description of what he had found at number 7 Kingsgate, through his indignation and fear at being thought in any way responsible, to the final, quite fluent analysis of his feelings for Jo.

Then he steeled himself for Tony's comments and questions. His vicar remained silent for some moments and then asked, 'What was that wonderful piece you were playing in church this afternoon? Not the quiet one but the one you were beginning on when I had to go.'

Profoundly thankful to escape from the present horrific reality into the insulating safety of his obsession, Cavill hastened to explain. 'It's a sortie by a Frenchman, Lefebvre-Wely. That's what you call a piece to drown the congregation's noisy exodus. That one was the E-flat. Like me, he was a church organist but he earned his living as a concert player, which was a bit easier in his day. After his death he was frowned on by some people for being too popular but now he's creeping back into fashion. The boys call it my fairground music because the sequences are audacious and the cadences sometimes quite absurd – a bit like the rhymes in Browning's poetry. You know, there's no reason why it shouldn't be done like that, but who else would have dared?

'There's another parallel piece. They'll make a startling ending to each half of a pretty heavy programme for my audience in Cologne next month – always providing I get one – so I'm practising them hard.'

'It didn't sound as though you needed to.'

Cavill corrected him almost cheerfully. 'Sorry to sound rude, but the Cologne audience will be rather more discriminating than you.'

'I bet they won't. I bet half of them will have come to be seen at the concert. They won't have any better an ear than mine to appreciate your skill. They'll have accepted your reputation on the recommendation of their betters.'

Smiling, Cavill got up to go. 'Ah, but I'll be playing for the other half.' He tried to put his finger on how, in less than twenty minutes, Tony had managed to make him feel normal again, not happy but certainly human.

Tony groped in a drawer for his car keys. 'Later, you'll want to talk further but you need some sleep first. Come back when you're ready. I'll run you home now.' They drove the short distance in silence.

As Cavill stood at his front door, key in hand, Tony

wound down his car window. 'I'm certainly not expecting you to be fit for duty tomorrow morning. Have a lie-in. If the choir won't sing unaccompanied, we'll say the service.'

Cavill shook his head. 'I'll only get through tomorrow by concentrating on all my normal duties. I'll play the E-flat sortie for you at the end of the service. With luck, the more discriminating of my choir members will find fault with my execution of it.'

Mitchell wondered how literally Browne had meant his one-drink-only warning and how soon he could call his DCI's bluff. He stood and fished in his pocket for money. When he saw the inspector's right eyebrow meet up with the unruly tuft of hair that always fell forward over his brow, he knew that he was safe.

Browne's tone, though, was severe. 'So long as it's purely to ensure that your voice lasts out long enough to convey all your profound thoughts.'

Mitchell grinned. 'It's more because the first one went down without touching the sides.' As he queued, he mulled over the scant information Browne had given them and prepared his thoughts, profound or otherwise, ready for fluent delivery when Browne should call on him.

Refusing to be specific about times of death, Ledgard had offered two certain facts. First, only one of the girls, Jo Merry, had been killed in the chair where she had been found. Second, there was a period of round about twenty-four hours separating the first killing from the last. When the police doctors had arrived, Jo Merry's body had still been virtually at its normal temperature. They and Browne had considered briefly, even at this stage, whether they were hunting a psychopath. They feared so.

Dr Ledgard had pointed out that the girls' clothing was intact and that there had been no obvious ritual markings. Nothing so far as he could see had been removed as a memento – they all still had both shoes and both earrings, for instance. Nor had excess violence been used. Sufficient to ensure that they were dead, of course, but these were not frenzied killings. On the other hand, three girls had been killed elsewhere and the four of them brought together and arranged in a macabre imitation of a social gathering. Not the average murderer's method of covering his tracks.

When Mitchell placed his tray of glasses on their table, the scene of the crime was still the topic of conversation. 'If three of them were killed in the previous twenty-four hours, it's likely that none of it happened in that house. So why should he gather them there in particular?'

Browne shook his head. 'There doesn't have to be a reason – at least, not the sort that we understand. The question I'm asking myself, Jennie, is whether killing Jo Merry was our customer's grand finale, so that she could be a late hostess to her late guests, or a last-minute adaptation of his former plan to leave her three bodies to account for when she arrived home.'

Jennifer answered Browne's question with another. 'I wonder, sir, if you'd mind calling me Jennifer?'

Browne blinked. 'I wouldn't mind, but I'm not sure, in the heat of the moment, that I'll remember.'

She blushed and returned to their speculation. 'It's as if he was making a statement about how clever he'd been, showing them off. It would have given him longer to cover his tracks if he'd left the bodies scattered around to be found separately. He seems pretty confident that we won't get on to him very easily.'

Mitchell handed a pint tankard to his father-in-law. 'Isn't that another pointer to a psycho? And I was wondering about the other girl, Ruth Somebody. Was he out to get her or did he know she'd be away? By the way, have the bridesmaid's parents been asked to ID the non-resident?'

Browne nodded an acknowledgement of his beer. 'Slow down. I've forgotten what the first question was.'

'Doesn't matter. They're all rhetorical.'

Mitchell scowled amiably at his fellow sergeant. 'The last one wasn't.' He waited for the spat to develop but Jennifer had opted out again and retreated behind her pint. That too was an innovation. Formerly, her tipple had been shandy, in halves. He shrugged and turned back to Browne.

'They're being brought over tonight. If the fourth girl isn't Briony Cocker, then the chances are we have a fifth corpse lying around somewhere.'

'Thanks for nothing. So, back to finding out why they all ended up having a coffee party in Kingsbury.'

Mitchell disposed of half his pint in a swallow. 'Three of them lived there.'

'But they didn't die there, so why collect them up?' Jennifer was sipping abstemiously as she reconsidered. 'Actually, we don't know that they weren't killed there. It wasn't a messy death for any of them, so we'll be hard-pressed to prove where it did happen. Was that why he chose strangling? And so that his little tableau would be aesthetically pleasing? Maybe he was crazy enough to pick them just because they were nicely contrasting types to make up an interesting group. Perhaps he had no other reason to wish harm to any of them.'

'You mean they should have felt flattered to be chosen?' Mitchell rolled his eyes.

They fell into silence, companionable at first but, after some moments, rather uncomfortable. Browne broke it with the suggestion that the best way they could move the case forward at this point was to snatch an early night whilst sleep was still on their daily agenda, and whilst they waited for the information they needed.

'Oh, but . . .'

Browne saw that Jennifer had pulled her wallet from her bag. He grinned. 'I suppose the equality of women is your excuse to insist on another round.'

Jennifer's head jerked up, startling both men. 'Do you have a problem with that?'

Mitchell was surprised into silence. Browne merely shook his head. 'Not with yours being the next round. I do think, though, that we should defer the pleasure.

We've ground to a halt for want of information that will put us on the right track. Some of it will be available tomorrow. We'll grab our rest while we can.'

'Sir.' Jennifer's face was expressionless as she slipped her purse back into her bag.

Browne's tone remained even. 'Their local police have informed the next of kin of the girls' deaths where possible. I shall hear tonight whether or not we have found Briony Cocker. Dr Ledgard tells me the PMs on two of the girls will be done tomorrow. On a Sunday too! There seem to be just a few advantages in having four corpses on our hands.'

Virginia was surprised to hear Benny's key in the door so soon after ten o'clock. She was comfortably settled in a much-sponged and somewhat battered armchair with a jazz concert on the radio and one infant firmly plugged to each side of her chest. She switched off the radio but small glugging sounds punctuated the brief marital conversation.

Mitchell filled the kettle and made himself generally useful as he offered his news. 'You'll never guess who's on the case with us.'

'I don't need to. She rang me up.'

'You never said!'

'It was after you'd gone. She got to the pub before you and Dad so she talked to me while she waited.'

'Did she sound odd to you?'

Virginia considered. 'Yes, a bit.' She passed their younger daughter to her father for burping and performed the same service herself for their younger son. 'She announced herself as Jennifer and put me off very politely when I asked her round here. Still, with a spree killer on the loose she won't be expecting to have much free time. She gave me a message for you. I've to tell you she didn't mean to be rude this afternoon.' She chuckled. 'I usually have to say that about you rather than to you about someone else.' She laid her son in his carrycot and made tea with the water her husband had boiled. 'Did your pub session get everything sorted?'

'Not even *anything*. It didn't achieve your father's real purpose either.'

'Which was?'

'To get us all three back on the old footing before the work really begins. I don't think it's going to be like that again. Jennie - sorry, Jennifer - isn't the same. She doesn't even look the same. It took me several seconds even to recognize her. What's happened to her? She used to answer to anything, the ruder the better.'

'A lot's happened. She's lost a husband and she's got two small daughters to raise without a partner to share the responsibility. I know she has Paul's mother here in Cloughton and her own parents on the other end of a phone, but they're a different generation. It's not—'

'Yes, I can see it's not the same - but the old Jennie would have coped.' His voice was muffled as he bent to arrange his daughter at the opposite end of the cot to her twin.

'Well, if she doesn't come to me, the babies and I will have to go to her and then we'll see. I'm not sure what I'd be like with this crew to care for on my own.'

Mitchell grinned complacently. Surely she wasn't fishing for a compliment? 'What's for supper?' he demanded.

Barry Parker was not fond of lying in bed, unless, of course, he had a woman lying beside him. In any case, since his two younger sons had become choristers at St Barnabas', Sunday breakfasts were no longer late and lazy. He accepted the unhealthy plateful of fried oddments that his second wife allowed and cooked for him once a week, but his pleasure in it was marred by her tart expression.

'Stephanie didn't come in last night.'

He shrugged and picked up his knife and fork. 'She's eighteen. There's not much I can do about it.' Why were the children that he'd fathered to Beryl such a problem? Paul and Benjie were completely different, normal. They liked football and TV cartoons and never mooched about sulkily as Steff and Jon had done even when they were quite small.

He supposed Debbie must be a better mother. In some ways she was a better wife, too – and he could manage for the rest. He was determined to hang on to this marriage. Debbie would never let him have Paul and Benjie if he beggared off from her. She wasn't exciting exactly, but she was a good housekeeper and she never moaned like Beryl had done.

He made appreciative noises at her between mouthfuls of bacon, wondering as he chewed where Steff was likely to be. Not that he was going to take her to task. She could put the boot in good and proper if he got on the wrong side of her.

Everyone would blame him, of course, though even as a six-year-old Steff had asked for it. Naturally, he hadn't given it her until she was twice that age. He wasn't a monster. And she'd wanted it quite as much as he did.

He gave Debbie a squeeze as she passed him to pour milk on the boys' cereal. 'Only half a slice of fried bread. Does that mean I can have toast and marmalade?'

'Oh, go on then.' Debbie trotted good-naturedly back to the kitchen.

Steff had probably spent the night with that black beggar again. With a bit of luck she'd move in with him soon, and if she did, he'd make sure it wasn't convenient for her to move back here again. He pushed aside his greasy and crumb-covered plates and regarded his younger sons complacently as they shovelled cornflakes into wide-open mouths. 'Fancy a kick-around in the park when your breakfast's gone down a bit?'

They replied in chorus. 'It's church this morning!'

They even looked pleased about it. Certainly, for some reason, Debbie approved of them going. 'Well, this afternoon then?' They nodded and Barry was satisfied. His second family was well worth sacrificing an hour at the pub for. And he wouldn't let Steff spoil it. Anyway, if what he had heard was right, she was soon going to have more to worry about than putting her dad's nose out of joint.

Chapter Seven

Mitchell always enjoyed the first briefing on a new case. From the rawest constable to the DCI or superintendent in charge, everyone felt that here was a fresh chance to make good, to be the one who noticed or deduced that vital something that tracked down their villain and put another star against his or her own name. The procedures were familiar but the personalities and circumstances of the victims and the suspects were new. At this early stage there was even a hint of indignation on the victims' behalf, of concern for their close relations, of a desire for justice to be done.

As usual, he was the first of the summoned officers to arrive, though Jennifer Taylor followed close on his heels. He had dropped automatically into the most comfortable of the available seats in Browne's office, and rose quickly to offer it. When Jennifer affected not to notice and settled herself on a bentwood chair beside Browne's desk, Mitchell gave up. She could come round in her own good time.

He looked around at the remainder of the current team who had quickly assembled behind them. Since

Browne was still shuffling his notes, they were exchanging wild and wonderful theories about the killer and his victims. Mitchell suspected that the DCI's papers were already in pristine order and that he was merely playing with them as he listened to the idle chat and gauged the mood of his men. When he looked up, silence fell.

Browne grinned and addressed them without reference to his notes. 'I'm glad to hear you aren't short of original ideas, but, for the moment, we'll keep to the facts, which are few. Four girls are dead, by strangulation with a ligature, the same one for all of them. It appears to be some kind of chain with fairly big links, maybe the sort of thing used to hang up heavy mirrors or pictures.

'We have identified all the victims. Last night, the parents of Briony Cocker confirmed that the fourth dead girl is their daughter. They have no idea what she might have been doing in Miss Merry's house. Actually, they seemed to have no knowledge of any part of her life as a student.' Mitchell grinned to himself. Browne had had less knowledge than he believed about Ginny's Oxford life before it had been cut short by her pregnancy.

Browne cleared his throat. 'In this case, more than most, we need to know what the experts can tell us. Dr Ledgard will perform at least one PM for us this morning and the SOCO boys have done their stuff at the house. Superintendent Petty agrees that more manpower is imperative, but we'll have to start without it this morning. There's one more thing. When Dr

Ledgard was presented with four bodies to examine he shared with us a few thoughts on multiple killers . . .'

'It's his hobby, reading up on them.'

'Yes, Benny. He reminded me that most start off with a minor sexual offence, the importance of which is seldom acknowledged at the time . . .'

'We've got one, haven't we? The Parker lad.' This time, Mitchell sounded reluctant rather than smug.

He had at least stimulated Jennifer to make a contribution. 'I thought we were sticking to facts. The only connection we've got so far between that boy and the four girls is the fact of his disappearance and their deaths in the same week. It could be that whoever killed the girls has killed him.'

Browne nodded. 'You've spoken to his mother, Benny. What did you make of what she told you?'

Mitchell attempted an impartial view. 'Painted doll. She was good at the blameless and inconsolable parent bit. She obviously doesn't give a toss about him.' Mitchell was pleased with himself. Quite objective, really. Well, he hadn't called her a cow. 'She'd no idea where he'd been when he'd gone off before and she couldn't say who his friends were. Not having met any of them, she was quite sure they were undesirable. It's unusual that when the father left he took both children with him. I wonder if they wanted to go? And why should he have wanted to take them?'

'And why should his new woman have wanted to take them in?' When no one else volunteered, Jennifer attempted to answer her own question. 'Maybe the first Mrs Parker's "one slip" was a serious commitment.

She might have wanted a new start with a new man and no strings. Children don't like being unwillingly tolerated.'

She was speaking directly to Mitchell, but he was busy fishing in his pocket to produce two postcard-sized photographs. 'This is him.'

Jennifer accepted and studied them. Vulnerable was the first word that sprang to her mind. 'He's attractive, handsome even. He doesn't look twenty.' In the picture his mother had provided the boy was smiling, but tentatively. In the police shot, the brows were drawn together over eyes dark and inward-looking, their expression closed. His hair was thick but lank, the chin and mouth like a child's. She laid both pictures on the desk and addressed Mitchell again. 'Where do you think he is?'

Mitchell shrugged. 'No idea, but he'll turn up when he's good and ready; when his mother, whatever her attitude, is rattled and he can manipulate her again.'

'So you think he's a spoiled brat?'

'I think he probably feels he has nowhere to belong and he deserves some sympathy for that, but it doesn't necessarily make him likeable or innocent. I'd like to pull his details out of the records and see exactly what he's been up to.'

'We could get his probation officer in on it.' Jennifer was beginning to sound enthusiastic. 'And hear the story of the original offence from the sister's point of view. I find it very difficult to reconcile rape with playing the organ.'

'Why?'

Browne held his breath at Mitchell's aggressive tone but Jennifer seemed to respond to his antagonism better than to his attempts to conciliate. 'I hadn't stopped to work it out, but organ-playing is so civilized and rape so brutal – and, well, the organ has churchy overtones.'

'On that note,' Browne suggested, 'perhaps we'd better consider Mr Jackson. He discovered the bodies, he had some sort of attachment to one of the victims, and to treat four dead people to a piano recital is a bit eccentric to say the least.'

Mitchell felt reluctantly compelled to add: 'He said he'd not touched the bodies. As far as he can recall, he only walked over to the piano. It's difficult to imagine, unless he was quite certain the girls were dead, why he didn't at least look for signs of life in Jo Merry. And how could he be certain unless he was responsible?'

Browne nodded. 'Anything else arising out of your talk with him last night?'

Mitchell said, deprecatingly, 'Only a lot of questions. I couldn't go along with his theory that one postgraduate student and three undergrads could club together out of their grants to pay the mortgage on a house that probably cost at least a couple of hundred thousand. Then, Jackson said that Ruth Roberts's boyfriend was playing in the concert they were going to, that he'd conned them all into buying tickets. So why was Ruth conveniently miles away while all the mayhem was going on?'

Into the silence that followed, a DC spoke up from the back of the room. 'Perhaps Jo Merry has a solicitor we could talk to.' Mitchell was grateful to him, well aware that he had done more than his share of talking. When Browne handed out their action sheets he was unsurprised to find that he was working in tandem with Jennifer, but startled to find that their first port of call was to be the mortuary.

As Mitchell adorned his person with the protective clothing Dr Ledgard had supplied, he tried to work out why Browne had absented himself from this crucial PM. He thought he had already fathomed the reason why he had sent Jennifer and himself along. Having failed to recreate the old atmosphere in a pleasant, social milieu last evening, he was probably now hoping that the two of them would become fellows in adversity in the morgue. He was sure Jennifer would have no trouble coping with what she would see. It couldn't be a first time for her, though he could not recall their ever having attended a PM together. He tried and failed to imagine her needing or seeking his own support.

Personally, Mitchell had few qualms. He greatly appreciated the pleasures of using and abusing his own body, and enjoyed a post-mortem partly because it added to his understanding of how all the parts of it functioned. There was just one brief detail of Ledgard's procedure that always repelled him. He endured the smell philosophically, and hearing the knife parting the flesh. It was the same sound as when his barber sawed his scissor blades through thick clumps of his hair. Each organ was carefully cut free, precisely placed and minutely examined. But then, the essentials over, Ledgard scraped everything into a black plastic bag, plonked it inside the body and just patted it level before leaving his minions to sew up his incisions. Mitchell silently protested at the indignity whilst perfectly understanding the time-wasting pointlessness of painstaking replacement.

Without looking at her, he was aware that Jennifer showed no reaction to any of Ledgard's activities. He supposed women were well adjusted to coping with the messier aspects of life. Was this, he wondered, why the Almighty had elected them to be responsible for childbearing, or was it the other way round? Had the birth process toughened women up? He considered Jennifer's case in particular, though he was not sure that toughening was the process she had gone through.

Had she changed for good? Could she still be in shock after her husband's fatal accident two years ago? The two of them had helped one another over many a difficult moment in the past, not by offering mutual sympathy but by doing some straight talking whenever each had felt the other deserved it. They had parted two years ago with regret and mutual respect. Now he felt tongue-tied. Unusually for him, he didn't feel he could put his finger on what was wrong. If the girl was simply grieving he would just have to be patient.

Mitchell had never liked Paul Taylor. After Jennifer had married him, their good honest professional relationship had continued unspoiled, but the Taylors, as a pair, had not been part of the Mitchells' social circle as the former Jennie Smith had been.

He dismissed her temporarily from his mind and concentrated on what Dr Ledgard had to tell them. Briony Cocker had been dead long enough for rigor to have passed away fully. When Ledgard had examined the body yesterday it had passed only from the face and neck muscles. Mitchell frantically calculated. 'So Briony must have been killed very soon after she had left the Staniforths' house to meet her friend?'

'Some friend,' Ledgard grunted as he divested himself of his working gear to reveal a many-hued sweater and balding cord trousers. 'The foetus was eleven to twelve weeks. Tell Tom I'll get the report to him this afternoon. Will he be here after lunch for the next one?'

Jennifer shook her head. 'I don't know. He's called us for a second briefing at one o'clock. I won't be here. I've to go over the house. I'm not sure where lunch fits in.'

Mitchell opened the outer door with a flourish. 'How about now, in the Fleece? There's nearly an hour before we're due back to barracks. Your treat, since you didn't get your round in last night!'

Jennifer gave Mitchell the first grin since they had been reacquainted. 'You'll have a price limit then, and that will include the beer.'

The Clough Road allotment-holders had been delighted to hear that Kenneth Benson had taken on plot number 18 and approved of his stout intention to tackle the tangle of rampant dock, dandelion and couch grass as soon as conditions allowed. The weekend had been damp and comparatively mild and Ken had decided to make a start on turning over the ground, so that the next freeze-up would work for him, breaking the clods of clay down further.

For most of this Sunday morning he had worked with a will and considered he had earned his beef and Yorkshire pudding. He wiped the worst of the yellowish mud off his spade with grass and dock leaves. Soon he must sort out that serviceable little shed in the corner, but for now he shouldered his spade and took it away with him.

He looked back, and his spirits fell a little as he observed how small a portion of the total task his two hours of hard work represented. Then he trailed rather disconsolately along the cinder track that separated the odd-numbered plots from the even. As he squeezed himself and his spade through the kissing gate at the end, he raised a hand in salute to an approaching figure.

It was Sam, who tended the largest and best-ordered plot on the lower side of his own. Sam grinned. 'Just come to oppen't greenhouse winders a crack. Coming down this aff?' Ken nodded. ''Appen I'll give you a bit of an 'and. Yon's a bit dauntin' for one. I'll get me reward in't summer when your dandelion seeds aren't blowin' across my veg. See yer.'

Ken walked on with renewed energy and an increased appetite for his Yorkshire pudding.

*

At Family Eucharist in St Barnabas' Church, the central heating, together with the sun that was laying warm patches of colour on all the surfaces in line with the windows, gave an illusion of summer. It was not borne out by the floral arrangements, the vicar observed. The ladies had done their utmost as usual but the chrysanthemums were past their best now, whilst the forced spring blossoms seemed offended at having to perform before they were ready. They had no place in this dead, after-Christmas time when everything was in tatters, from the stripped and needleless trees resting by his congregation's dustbins to their broken New Year's resolutions, languishing God knew where.

Tony tried to shake off his low spirits. Cavill had been playing magnificently. His voluntary, some rather stirring piece, had not been very conducive to the examination of one's heart and mind before making one's Communion, but it was ideal for shutting out the horrors of his last twenty-four hours. He had made no comment on Tony's change of opening hymn. 'New Every Morning' had not seemed a tactful choice.

'Redeem thy misspent time that's past.
Live each day as if 'twere thy last . . .'

Excellent advice but a terrifying warning. He wondered first how the four girls had spent theirs, and then how many of his congregation were aware of the four killings and their choirmaster's connection with them. Perhaps he should make a reference to it, make the remarks in his sermon relevant to it – or, perhaps not.

Having read the Gospel from the chancel steps, he left his service book in the care of the head chorister and ascended to the pulpit. His sermon lay before him as he had prepared it yesterday, safely Blu-Tacked to the surface below, complete with its quips and witticisms. He smiled at his own vanity. Maybe he should preach on that. *Vanity of vanities . . . all is vanity.* He was fond of the book of Ecclesiastes. It often suited his mood. He decided on a revised and abbreviated version of what he had originally planned and began his address.

The congregation's subdued reception of it suggested to him that many of them were up to date with the local news. At least it would eclipse his own small fame as champion of the local traders.

'" . . . And now unto Him who is able to keep us from falling . . ."' Their instruction over, he watched the congregation shuffle themselves upright and led them smoothly into the Creed.

Mrs Kirkbride senior shook off her daughter's restraining hand and struggled defiantly to her feet with the rest, though she omitted to recite the real substance of her faith. It consisted of believing it to be her duty to set an example to her social inferiors, which she was presently fulfilling by following the traditional upper-middle-class habit of attending morning worship. Over and above her observation of this duty, she had obliged the Almighty by encouraging her only son to follow his uncle into the Church, rather than his father into the Army.

She sank thankfully on to her pew again as the congregation, having looked for the resurrection of the dead and life everlasting, stopped chanting. It was only just after eleven and already she felt exhausted. Suffering for and with Jean was draining. Why did they have to put her and themselves through it? The honest answer was because Di insisted.

As the intercessions were led by a member of the congregation, Mrs Kirkbride senior pondered on the closeness of her two offspring. It had not always been the case. Before Tony went away to theological college, they had fought bitterly. Perhaps distance had lent, if not enchantment, at least tolerance. Or, perhaps Diana, having been the twin of a stillborn sister, felt the need for a close relationship with a sibling.

Whatever the case, she had been grateful for the cessation of their noisy arguments, and now she willed Diana to come to a similar understanding with Tony's wife. Not that there was serious animosity between them. It was just that Jean needed constant reassurance and Diana had so little patience with those who lacked self-sufficiency. Mother and daughter knelt together to claim their rightful absolution for such sins as they were prepared to acknowledge.

Diana settled her mother as comfortably as an octogenarian could be settled in a kneeling position on a lumpy hassock. The old woman knelt stiffly upright, disdaining to support her buttocks on the pew seat, unlike Jean on the other side of her whose huge body overflowed on to it.

She sighed as she faced the difficulties of the day ahead. She could find no way to convince her sister-in-law of the gratitude she felt to her for Tony's comfortable life. Jean had labelled her a snob and insisted on keeping her at arm's length.

She wondered why she had condemned herself to these seventy minutes of boredom and discomfort. The pressures of upper-middle-class tradition, she supposed. Pressures felt by her mother, not herself. An occasional attendance at Matins wasn't, after all, much for her mother to ask of her. Not that it was Matins today, unfortunately, though she had certainly been rewarded by the music. Quite remarkable in such a run-down, working-class parish. She had come partly to please Tony. Certainly not to pay her respects to a God who had been so cruel to her.

Jean's confession began fervently and sincerely. Tony had tried to explain to her what was going wrong between her and his relatives. Instead of reaching out and responding to the person, she was retreating into her protective shell and merely offering them a polite little formula from the selection she had been taught. His family had been taught different ones and so neither side knew how to respond. Each labelled the other moody and criticized her for being difficult; 'not what we're used to'. But how did you reach out to a person except by showing them good manners? And had Tony told Diana to reach out to his wife? She suspected not. Had she been treating Cavill the same way? Is that why he hadn't confided in her about the murders last night?

By the time Jean's lips were promising 'newness of life to the glory of thy name', she had passed to reflecting on the Kirkbride family's housekeeping, which by Jean's standards was rather sloppy in spite of all their money and airs and graces.

The service proceeded to the anthem. What a lot of noise Cavill had been making. You'd never think he'd just lost the girl he was practically engaged to. And here he came, trotting out of the organ door to conduct his choir as though everything was normal.

Cavill thought no one but Tony and the choir members would be aware that the anthem had been changed as well as one lesson and two hymns. The Epiphany piece they'd practised would still be relevant next week, and 'These are they which follow the Lamb' was one of the anthems in their repertoire to be plucked out in an emergency. Cavill became cross when all Victorian church music was condemned as sentimental and vulgar. Goss was often simple and chaste. He was fairly sure that the text for the music was inapt for the four girls. Strictly speaking, it didn't apply even to Jo, but the atmosphere of this very short piece said what he felt he would like to say.

As he walked towards the music stand that his head chorister had set out for him, midway between the decani and the cantoris stalls, he scanned the pews at the back of the building. Occasionally, Jon would wander into a service towards the end and stay to listen to his voluntary before disappearing again. There was no sign of him. The anthem was rendered to his satisfaction and, after smiling approval at his probationer choirboy, he returned to the organ loft to play the last hymn.

Benjie Parker's cup was full. Mr Jackson had listened to him singing at this week's practice, and said he could join in parts of this morning's anthem if he was sure he knew them. Then it had changed to this one that he knew all the way through. He'd sung all of it, quietly, right in Reuben's ear.

It was Reuben's job to report everything about the service to Mr Jackson, especially his own behaviour. For the five weeks Benjie had been in the choir, he had been restricted, on Sundays, to sitting in the stalls and watching carefully so that he'd learn what to do in services, when to stand and sit and kneel. He'd done everything right today. Except that he'd stared round a bit during the sermon.

That old lady was in church again, the one with the horrible mole at the side of her mouth with hairs growing out of it. She was the vicar's mum. It was a good job Mr Kirkbride hadn't got any children or she'd have been their grandma and they'd have had to kiss her like he had to kiss Auntie Edith. She was his great-aunt, actually, and there were even more hairs on her mole. It was a shame because she made ace teas, and when he went there he could hardly swallow for thinking about having to kiss her when it was time to go home. He felt shivery now as he thought about those hairs tickling against his cheek, and he wriggled on his hard pew.

Reuben took his notebook and wrote 'Fidgeted' against Benjie's name. Benjie hated him.

Chapter Eight

Sunday's lunchtime briefing had lived up to its name and been brief. Browne had summarized the team's problems. There was so much to do, it was difficult to know where to begin. The macabre coffee party pointed to a killer whose sanity was at least in question. 'That doesn't mean he had no practical reason for getting rid of the girls, but it does suggest that the key to the case is the nature of the killer. Unfortunately, we have to begin at the other end, concentrating on the nature of the girls till we find something they had in common and that leads us to one man.'

'Are we sure we're looking for a man?'

Jennifer was not sure whether the question had come from Craig or Winters. Browne had hesitated only briefly before replying, 'Physically, a woman could have used the ligature, but considering the circumstances, I incline to concentrate on a man.' Jennifer agreed with him.

Benny had wriggled out of accompanying her to Kingsbury. He had convinced Browne that it would be a good idea to see what the vicarage family had to say about Jackson before speaking to him again. 'He did say Tony Kirkbride was his substitute father, and he'll be more inclined to tell the truth if he knows we've been checking up on him.'

Jennifer was quite glad to have a less dominating character for her companion as she examined number 7 Kingsgate and tried to recreate in her mind the girls' life there together. Not that Caroline Webster was by any means a nonentity. She was new since Jennifer had last worked in Cloughton, and had apparently wormed her way several times already into a CID investigation. Doubtless she hoped to join them officially before long.

She had certainly done her homework and shared her conclusions. 'This place is a long way out but it is on the right side of the city for the university. That little Fiat in the back lane is Marianne's. They probably travelled in that and shared the fuel costs. None of them seem to have been hard up.' The two women made a cursory tour of the downstairs rooms that had been examined already by the SOCO teams and Browne and Petty, before beginning a search of the bedrooms.

Jennifer was less offended by Paula's chaos than either Marianne or Jo had been. There were very few books amid the clutter, considering that the girl was supposed to have been studying for a degree. The only area of comparative order was the top of the dressing table. 'Estée Lauder will go bankrupt,' Caroline observed, 'now they've lost this lady's custom.' Jennifer smiled as they set about a systematic search.

It occurred to her that her own personal

circumstances, and the dramatic nature of the crime they were investigating, had prevented her coming to grips with the outrage of what had been done to the four young girls as individuals. Jo must, she supposed, be at least thirty, but even so the prime of her life had been stolen from her.

It had not fallen to Jennifer's lot to break the news of their relative's death to Briony's parents, nor to Marianne's father, disabled by MS and cared for by his younger daughter, a girl of sixteen. The PM on Briony had not aroused Jennifer's pity. A body in the morgue was a body. The person was somewhere else. Perhaps it was partly working with Benny that had made her so callous. His approach to his work was to set himself to catch the criminal. He was anxious that no one be allowed to get away with any offence. He liked 'nicking people'. Each case for him was a cross between a game and a vendetta.

Whilst most of this was perfectly true, Jennifer knew she was being unfair to Mitchell. She had seen him weep quite unashamedly over a dead child. She redirected her attention to a drawerful of Paula's expensive and impractical underwear.

In another quarter of an hour the two officers compared notes. What they had seen suggested that Paula had been well-off, vain and rather stupid. 'No handbag,' Caroline observed, 'unless the SOCO boys have it.'

Jo's room demonstrated considerably less self-indulgence. It was the largest of the four and was obviously used partly as a sitting room. An expensive-looking and sizeable desk had more than half of its drawers locked. The rest contained part of a typed thesis, sheaves of handwritten notes and a text entitled *The Ancrene Riwle* that appeared to be in a foreign language. The two officers spent longer in here but obtained less of a flavour of the room's occupant. Again, there was no handbag to be seen.

'Perhaps our friend did collect trophies!' Caroline's voice was triumphant.

Jennifer's was flat. 'Perhaps he also collected the keys that open these drawers.'

They passed to Marianne's room. It could hardly be called spartan since it contained the pretty and comfortable furnishings that Jo had provided, but she seemed to have added almost nothing of her own. Every surface was neat and clear, with the exception of the bedside table on which stood a postcard-sized, framed photograph. It showed a man in a wheelchair. He had thick hair, rather long, round a gaunt, lined face. Her father, presumably, and the girls on either side his daughters. Marianne's cold beauty looked barely more animated than it had done in death. She stood a little apart from the other two. The younger girl, with similar features and pale hair, was smiling and pretty and rested one hand on the man's shoulder.

For some time, Jennifer and Caroline opened drawers and cupboards, jotting down occasional notes. 'Handbag?' Caroline enquired, when all had been examined. Jennifer shook her head.

*

Refreshed by an excellent lunch, topped off by a couple of pints of best, Ken Benson had returned to his allotment to find that his friend, Sam, had not only remembered his promise of assistance but had already dug half a row of the unbroken ground. Hastily, he joined in the work, apologizing for his tardy return.

Sam was sanguine. 'Don't fret. Doesn't do to upset the missus of a Sunday dinner.' They worked solidly for more than an hour, neither of them wasting breath on conversation. Then Sam paused, easing his lower back muscles, and wiped his brow with a khaki handkerchief that would have done duty as a tablecloth. 'My missus said ter bring you fer a brew at half-three. She's made fruit cake.'

Ken needed no second invitation, expressing profuse thanks both for the hospitality and for Sam's efforts with the spade. Both of them regarded the patch of worked ground with pride. 'Do another half-hour, mebbe, when we're rested. Ground might freeze up again any time.' Sam stumped off towards the shed on his own plot.

'Do you think,' Ken asked, 'that I could put my spade in there with yours till we come back?'

'Surely. You want to get a lock fer yer own. It's a good little shed, yon.'

'It's got one already. That's the problem. I don't know who has the key. It's not been returned to any of the council people who do the letting. I've asked them.'

'Eyup!' Sam looked puzzled and ambled away to see for himself. 'S'funny, that theer weren't there last time I looked. Tommy left it empty and oppen when 'e packed in.'

'There's a load of boxes inside,' Ken offered. Both men peered through the grimy window.

'Them aren't Tommy's.' Sam spoke with certainty. 'Them 'as no business ter be there. Them want seein' into. We'll 'ave that brew first, then us'll be the ones as'll see into 'em.'

Denis Betts felt guilty for bringing his hard-pressed vicar into the hospital to offer him Sick Communion. He had made steady progress since his operation and he was sure he could manage to get to the hospital chapel by himself, even if it meant going in a wheelchair. It was just that he had spent each day since listening to Irene's moans about the trials and tribulations of looking after two small children in a partly decorated house. He needed to talk with someone who could deal with his resentment. He couldn't be a good churchwarden, feeling as he did towards her. Certainly, he couldn't take Communion from the hospital chaplain with it all unresolved.

He was thankful but not surprised when Tony seemed to understand his dilemma and absolved him from his indignation, even bitterness perhaps, against his wife. Tony shared with him his own experiences that day at the vicarage and made 'the wife' a problem they shared. 'Jean can't cope with strong personalities like Di. She gets very uptight when they visit and her efforts not to hold it against me aren't very successful.'

He grinned at his warden. 'They can't help it. They're only women.'

When they had enjoyed this wicked joke, Tony became serious again. 'You don't want to be married to the perfect woman any more than I do. It would be crucifying. But to live with an imperfect one requires grace. Fortunately we can ask for that in large supplies. Just as our women can ask for it to help them cope with us.'

Much relieved, Denis had taken his Communion with a clear conscience. Now, only one worry remained. 'Did you manage to see Mr Oliver on Friday evening?'

'I did. He was fine, watching some game show on television and tucking into a good supper that a neighbour had brought in.' He chuckled. 'Said he couldn't remember the last time I'd been to see him. Jean thinks he pretends to be senile to manipulate us. I'm not sure. He'll probably tell you he sat through Friday all on his own and the kind neighbour will be as indignant as me.' He gathered up his belongings. 'Got to dash off now. I promised Jean if she coped till lunch was over and I'd been to see you, that I'd take Di for a walk till teatime to give her a break. I'd better go and do it.'

As he turned to raise his hand in farewell to his warden, a nurse in the corridor intercepted him. He was dismayed. He hated hospitals, had had to nerve himself, as always, in preparation for this visit. It wasn't, if he was honest, the dispirited atmosphere or even the imminence of death that put him off, so much as the demands made on his sympathy. He resented them, preferred to commiserate and condole voluntarily. A most reprehensible quality in a minister, but he doubted that there were many of his calling who, deep down, felt any differently.

He smiled at the nurse. Waited. Mrs Greenhow, she told him, had seen him from her side ward on his way in. She said she needed to speak with a minister. He smiled again, genuinely this time: off the hook.

'I know Mrs Greenhow. I was sorry to hear how ill she is, but it isn't me she means. She's a Methodist, attends the Field Lane church. Her minister is—'

'She said she wanted you.'

'There's your chaplain too. Mustn't tread on his toes.'

The nurse was shaking her head. 'I appreciate your scruples, but the chaplain's over the road in the children's ward and I don't know where the Methodist man is. Mrs Greenhow's just had her lungs drained again and feels a bit perkier, but she's nearer the end than she thinks. She might only have time to see you.'

He acquiesced. She led him silently to the bedside and left him. Tony stood at the foot of the bed, regarding the woman who lay against a heap of pillows. The hair was grey, white at the temples. The face was greyish too, deeply lined with straight furrows from nose to mouth, as though she had spent many years with her lips pursed. Below the chin, the skin hung in deep folds. Her expression, though, was placid, self-contained.

She stared back at him. 'What are you thinking, Vicar?'

'That you don't look as ill or as distressed as I expected.'

She smiled. 'I'm not distressed, but I am very ill. My doctors have fixed me up temporarily and I'm grateful.' She spoke firmly and sat forward.

Seeing the effort it cost her, he was alarmed. 'Be careful. You shouldn't . . .'

She silenced him with the flutter of a hand. 'Leave me be. If a woman has an ache or a pain she takes a pill and gets on with life. When you men get them, you build your social lives round them, assume special suffering voices, pained expressions. You dish out supporting roles in the drama to all the women who gather round. Women can't do with all that.'

She paused and drew a rasping breath as quietly as she could. Chastened, Tony tried again. 'What is it that I can do for you?' Maybe she wanted a temporary patching-up of her spiritual life to counterbalance the efforts of her physicians.

She was breathing more normally again. 'I want to tell you something and then to ask your advice. Mind you, I don't promise to take it.'

'That relieves me of a certain amount of responsibility.' He took a chair from a stack in the corner and brought it to the bedside. He admired her spirit. His sympathy was entirely voluntary.

'It was during the war.'

She paused for several seconds, leaving Tony unsure whether her bravado had exhausted her, or if she was having difficulty in bringing herself to make her confession. He tried to help. 'They were difficult times.'

'What would you know about it? There were compensations. Shared hardships could be put up with quite cheerfully.'

'Tell me about it then.'

'We had ways of getting round the shortages. I knew a Co-op where I could get six packets of cigs in exchange for ten milk tokens.' He thought she was deliberately misunderstanding him. 'We sifted the ashes of the night before's fire for nuggets of coal and we made balls of soap, melted and moulded from scraps.'

There was a half-smile on her lips. If she died among contented recollections without getting to her point, so what?

'We listened to "Kitchen Front" each morning – Freddy Grisewood giving hints and recipes. Very useful because I had to manage on just my rations. My job didn't leave time to queue when little extras came into the shops. In the evening, there was ITMA, and Jack Train . . .' She paused to get her breath again. He wondered whether to take her hand, decided she wouldn't appreciate it.

'You'd have been happy, Vicar. There was a huge increase in the numbers of churchgoers, all with devout-looking faces.' There was a longer pause. Her eyes were closed.

He prompted. 'It wasn't all good, though?'

She was lying back against the pillows now, her voice quiet but steady. 'My young husband was out when his call-up papers came. I opened the envelope and my knees gave way. He came in, glowing with the cold, and I had to give him the bad news. There was a postal order for his train fare. We talked quite cheerfully, but our fear filled the room. All he said was, "Will I still be able to practise my trumpet?" '

Tony watched the tears roll down the emaciated cheeks and waited, respecting her grief till she rallied. 'I saw him just twice again. The end of his life came suddenly. I'm dragging my ending out. We all get there different ways. I didn't choose mine but there's comfort in the certainty of it. I won't fail to pull it off.'

It occurred to him that she was more qualified to counsel the dying than he was. Her breathing was noisy again. He felt she was shut off from him and wondered whether she had gone to sleep. Should he leave her in peace or would she be upset if she woke, still unburdened? He gazed out of the window until her voice startled him, strong again.

'Better get on with it. I've been told straight that I might be counting my time in hours.' She eyed him solemnly. 'One night, in the middle of an air raid, I stole a healthy baby boy that I'd delivered to a feckless, dirty, drunken prostitute and gave it to a caring, cultured, middle-class woman whose baby had been born dead.'

Tony kept his face and voice expressionless. 'I take it the real mother didn't know.'

'Neither mother knew. They were both high on gas and air and then sleeping it off. When I'd delivered him, his sluttish mother was still blind drunk. I wasn't leaving a newborn child with her. There were no special baby-care units. The hospital was full of wounded soldiers so I took the poor mite home till the raid was over.

'Then I delivered the dead baby, a little girl. Her mother had longed for her. She'd had three miscarriages and she was well turned thirty. What would you have done in my shoes?' She chuckled. 'Low-heeled, laced-over-the-instep granny shoes that made me look older and wiser than I felt.'

The voice had become faint but settled. 'I brought the sleeping child from my house and put him in the freshly painted second-hand cot. Even very much wanted first babies couldn't have everything new in forty-two. When the mother stirred, I helped her sit up to look at him. There was a photograph on the bedside table. I brought it close to the child and said, "He's just like your husband, isn't he?" I settled them both down and went off to follow what would have been the proper procedure if the drunk had given birth to a dead child.'

The old woman was exhausted now. She gave Tony a ghastly, skeletal grin. 'I'd have been a dab hand at the warming-pan in the bedchamber game, wouldn't I? I was born in the wrong century. For a while, I worried that the child would grow up to be the image of his father, whoever that might have been. I watched fearfully from a few streets away but no one suspected a thing. If anyone had found out I'd probably have been put in prison, but I'd do it all over again.'

'So, if you don't feel guilty, why are you telling me about it now?'

'Well, I'm not much longer for this world. It's now or never.'

'And you're wondering if you'll go to hell if you die with it unconfessed? I don't believe in a God who condemns mistakes made from pure motives.'

She gave him a faint smile. 'It's not going to hell I'm worried about. I've been a good Methodist all my life but it sounds to me as if hell's got to be more fun than harps and crowns. I'm just worried about the man's right to know who he really is. It's his last chance.'

Tony got up and took a turn round the tiny ward, weighing up the situation. Was the old woman in any state to examine her motives? Was she wanting this man, whoever he was, to be grateful to her for his comfortable upbringing? She wasn't likely to live long enough to enjoy his gratitude.

He walked back to the side of the bed. Mrs Greenhow looked weak, physically wasted, but somehow at peace with herself, not like someone on the horns of a tricky moral dilemma. He felt she was somehow using him, but he was not sure how much of an interrogation she could withstand. He dropped on to the chair again and this time he did take her hand. 'Have you thought,' he asked her, 'about what this man might lose if the truth came out now?'

He'd better try to persuade her to part with the

poor bloke's name. He would have to offer him some kind of support, he decided, if he couldn't persuade this amazing lady to leave well alone. 'Are you proposing to tell just the man, to leave the mother and family still deceived? It's not nearly as simple as you've made it sound . . .'

Suddenly, she was fighting for breath, her face mottled, blue and grey. Tony stuck his head into the corridor and shouted for help. Sister and a nurse appeared at once, inserted tubes, shouted into telephones. Tony was bundled unceremoniously out of the way.

Chapter Nine

Detective Constables Craig and Winters had had their fill of house-to-house enquiries. They had had their fill too of cakes, buns and biscuits, tea and coffee which the influential and respectable householders in Kingsbury had offered as tokens of their support of these bastions of law and order.

'Do they think,' Craig demanded, rhetorically, 'that paunchy coppers with bad teeth will do a better job? Or are they offering what they think people of our class like and expect? They wouldn't feed their children like that!' He kicked morosely at the station car-park gravel, then looked around guiltily to see if anyone had noticed the pebble that flew up and removed a chip of enamel from Jennifer's scarlet Fiesta. He caught Winters's eye. 'Canteen?' he suggested, hastily.

Winters looked surprised. 'What, for more stodge? Well, I suppose it's the last place we're likely to run into the CI. OK. At least it'll be warm.' But Winters heard Browne as they entered the stifling food hall.

'Just looking for me with your reports, were you?' Browne gave his DCs a sweet smile. 'You'll be glad to hear I've another exciting job for you. You'd better take a short break in here so that you're up to it. Coffee's as dire as usual but the doughnuts are worth killing for.'

Winters waited to note down Browne's instructions whilst Craig queued at the counter. When he brought his tray to the table where Winters was waiting, it held two coffees with cream and two doughnuts. He met his colleague's grin without flinching. 'If you don't want it, I'll have yours. Where are we off to?'

'To do a spot of gardening. Wasn't there any milk?'

'I'll drink your coffee too if it doesn't suit,' Craig offered, amiably. 'I'm allergic to gardening.'

Winters too felt less than keen when he saw the expanse of yellow mud he would have to cross to reach the shed where Ken Benson and Sam awaited them. He tucked the ends of his trouser legs into his socks before leaving the cinder track.

Benson was apologetic as he explained the circumstances of their call. 'The stuff's been there several days at least. I suppose I should have realized it had no business here but I didn't look very carefully. It's a nice weatherproof shed. It might well have been full of things the previous tenant hadn't room for at home.' He saw that Sam, left out of the conversation, was looking mutinous. 'It was – er . . .' He paused, realizing that he had not yet enquired after his benefactor's surname. 'It was Sam here who saw that some of the boxes are new and unopened and probably aren't here for any good purpose.'

Winters nodded and devoted his energies to picking the lock. Craig was not overexcited by the find. There were, as far as he could make out, only a couple each of television sets and video recorders. The other cartons looked older and probably genuinely contained stored household items and small gardening tools. The previous tenant, Tommy, had possibly been a small-time thief.

He made tactful enquiries of Sam, who scratched his upper lip with a muddy finger, thereby painting in a lopsided moustache that almost matched his hair. 'He give up because of 'is rheumatics, 'bout the middle of last winter, but 'e's kept on with 'is rent because he thought the better weather would help 'im.' He shook his head sorrowfully. 'He niver got goin' though, so 'e give up for good, end of November.'

'He won't have been in any state to have lifted these, then?'

Sam spluttered indignantly.

'Does he drive a hatchback or a van of some sort?'

Sam was crosser than ever. 'Them's stolen goods and Tommy 'asn't driven 'em nowhere. You want to watch your mouth, young feller.'

Winters, having mastered the lock, came to soothe him. Craig, realizing he was never going to be forgiven for this slur on Tommy's good name, wandered into the shed.

The window was fair-sized but the light was beginning to fade. Craig fished in his pocket for the small torch he always carried and prised open the interlaced top flaps of a large and scruffy cardboard carton with a couple of biros. Torchlight was reflected back from ribbed, knitted fabric. Socks? The biros were employed again and silver gleamed as the protective knitwear was drawn back.

He stepped aside to allow his colleague to take his place. Chris Winters had been pulled off the Heath Lees house raids to join the murder team, *and* he seemed to know a fair bit about antiques and suchlike. He'd know what to look for. As Winters probed delicately in the depths of a box, Craig prowled restlessly behind a pile of them till his foot caught in a piece of rope and he stooped to disentangle it. He fished for the torch again. It wasn't rope.

'Hey!' He stood up, both hands full and peered at Winters over the pile of boxes between them. 'Our chap's not only a burglar, he's a bag-snatcher as well.'

The phone on Browne's desk rang as Mitchell and Jennifer were leaving his office after presenting their reports. He signalled to them to remain as he listened to Magic Powers's news. James Enright had met Ruth Roberts at the station. She was very shocked to hear of the deaths of her fellow residents and the pair had presented themselves at the station. Was Ruth allowed to go on living in Kingsgate? Did the police wish to speak to her?

Browne imparted this information to his detective sergeants. 'You can talk to Enright now, Benny, before the two of them can cook up any more stories than they have already.'

Jennifer glared from the doorway. 'I suppose that leaves me to do the all-girls-together bit. Give you the woman's angle, then get lost while you clever men solve the case.' Catching Browne's eye, she stopped speaking. She did not apologize but stared at a point beyond his right shoulder.

'I thought I'd talk to Miss Roberts myself,' Browne's tone was businesslike, even amiable. 'I think you might benefit from an hour or so's study of the file, Sergeant Taylor. Then at least somebody on the case will be up to date with it. Off you go!' He turned to Mitchell. 'Bring them up, will you? I'll have Miss Roberts in my office – and could you send me Caroline? Find yourself a PC as a scribe and take Enright to Jerry's old corner of the general office.'

Browne took an almost instant liking to Ruth Roberts. She was that rare thing in his experience, a woman who could admit her own shortcomings without seeming to angle for a refutation of their existence. She settled herself neatly in the chair opposite him, knees and feet together. She seemed to have herself well in hand, regarding him gravely but offering no exhibition of tears and temperament.

'Would I be right in thinking you were not a particularly close friend of the dead girls?' he asked.

She considered the question carefully before replying. 'I was quite friendly with Jo. Paula and Marianne were younger. Paula was rather silly and I never met anyone that Marianne seemed very close to.'

'So you didn't get on with two of them?'

'I didn't say that. We had to live together and we all "got on" very well.'

'But the girls didn't confide in you?'

'As a matter of fact, they did sometimes. I was the only one who isn't pretty – well, the only one who accepted and admitted it – so I'm the one they all talked to. I wasn't considered a rival, so they told me their secrets. And what they didn't tell, it wasn't too difficult to work out for myself, at least as far as Paula was concerned.'

Browne considered Ruth had her own attraction, although he agreed that pretty didn't describe her. Her face was an exaggerated triangle, her hair dark, lying flat on her head in a manner that had not been fashionable since his mother's girlhood, and her brown eyes were enormous. She was thin to the point of emaciation but with a vigorous carriage. Not a physical presence he would forget in a hurry.

'Are you,' he asked her, 'prepared to share those secrets?'

It was manifest that the idea gave her no pleasure. She nodded once. 'In the circumstances, I suppose I'm going to have to. I'm the only person left who knows what went on in the house.'

'Take your time then.'

She looked down for some moments, then met his gaze again. 'I'm very sorry about what's happened. I heard about it on the radio this morning, but it was important to spend today with my mother and I didn't think what I had to tell you was so urgent that it wouldn't keep for twelve hours.'

'You had a particular reason for being at home today?'

'Yes, it's the second anniversary of my father's death. I didn't think of it last year, though I often thought about him, of course. Then, later, I noticed that my mother had circled it on the calendar. She'd done it again on this year's, so I arranged to spend the weekend with her.'

'In Nottingham?'

'That's right. I had to miss James's concert and he didn't understand why.'

'You didn't tell him, or he didn't think it a good enough reason?'

'The former. James and I had been living together and I couldn't decide whether to marry him. Living in Jo's house was a trial separation, thinking time. We still see each other from time to time. It would be difficult not to. But I didn't want, whilst we were separated, to go running to him with an explanation whenever I did what I wanted instead of what he did.'

'I see.'

Neither of them spoke for several seconds, then she sat back in her chair to appeal to him. 'Would you mind asking me some questions? I don't know where to begin.'

'And you don't want to reveal any unpleasant little secrets if they aren't relevant.' She smiled at him gratefully, till he added, 'I shan't know what's relevant till the case is over.'

'At least you could start me off.'

'Indeed I could.' He liked her more and more. 'We're

interested in your financial arrangements. We don't understand how four students on grants were putting together the mortgage payments on such a very expensive house.'

Ruth relaxed and as she smiled, two dimples appeared. 'That's easy. Jo didn't have a mortgage. The rents we paid were ludicrously small. That's why we didn't mind the transport costs into town. Jo didn't have us for our money. She had no relatives, at least none that she knew about. We were her substitute family.'

'So whose house is it?'

'Oh, it was Jo's, but she'd paid for it. She was very rich.'

'So where *did* her money come from? Mr Jackson led us to believe she was a student who had been brought up in a local children's home.'

The first tear appeared. Ruth ignored it and left it to find its way down the flat plane of her cheek and drip from her chin. 'That's right. Do you watch much television?'

'A policeman? No chance!'

'Well, there's a programme that's in its third series called "Blythe Spirit", like Noel Coward's play. Its heroine's called Joanna Blythe. It's a rags-to-riches story about an illegitimate girl who becomes a TV personality and gets everything she always sighed for and finds she doesn't really want it after all. I hope that last bit wasn't her own experience.' Ruth stopped and waited for Browne's conclusions to catch up. 'Joanna, Josephine. Blythe, Merry. Jo wrote the scripts, locked them in her desk till they were finished, then smuggled them to her producer.'

Browne deduced from Caroline's face that she was a devotee of the series and was kicking herself for not having made the connection between the names. He was not sure he would have made it himself. He turned back to Ruth. 'So why the secrecy?'

'She'd lived a life that made her secretive, but then there was Cavill.'

'Mr Jackson? Doesn't he approve of television soaps?'

'I don't suppose he cares one way or the other, but Jo was in love with him . . .'

'And wanted to know he wouldn't be marrying her for her money.'

'No. She didn't want him to refuse because of the money. She thought it would get in the way—'

'Just a minute!' Browne broke in against all his advice to his subordinates to give a witness her head if she was providing new and relevant information. 'He isn't stupid. He must have realized she was well off.'

Ruth smiled and nodded. 'It worked well at first. She bought the house from an old lady who had let it get a bit run-down. It seemed plausible that four girls should rough it, scrape together a mortgage. But then Jo began to earn more and more, and for most of her life she'd had so little. She couldn't resist lashing out and having everything as she wanted it. She just couldn't stop.'

'How did she know that Mr Jackson wouldn't have loved to have a rich wife?'

'You've met him.' The answer was sufficient. 'Anyway, none of it mattered. He liked her but you could tell that he didn't love her, not in the way Jo wanted. He'd never have married her. I don't think he's the marrying sort.'

'Do you know who gets it all now?'

Ruth shrugged. 'It didn't concern me. It certainly wasn't my place to ask.'

Browne nodded. 'What can you tell me about the girl who didn't live with you?'

'Briony? I don't know much at all. She was a friend of Paula's. I've met her once or twice. She wanted to take over my room, kept asking Paula when I'd be going back to James. She was pregnant.'

'That's right, about three months. Do you know who the father was?'

Ruth shook her head. 'No. Neither did she. According to Paula she was hovering between naming someone called Barry, who already had four children and didn't want to know, and another student called Sola. I've met him too, briefly. He's Nigerian but he was born in Birmingham. He was a friend of Paula's too. At one time he approached Jo about accommodation, so as to have Paula on hand and because Jo's terms were so reasonable. Jo refused. She didn't want the obvious complications of being a mixed household. Besides, there wasn't another spare bedroom and Paula's wasn't big enough to share. Sola, of course, accused Jo of racism.'

'But it wasn't that?'

'Definitely not. He didn't think so either. He was

just hitting out at her because he hadn't got his own way. They had a noisy argument one night. I heard him shout, "You don't want a dirty nigger lowering the tone of your high-class brothel, I suppose".'

'Brothel?'

Ruth bit her lip. 'He knew Paula was, well, not too fussy about . . . er . . . who she went about with. Actually, she was the one who defused the quarrel. He was highly amused when she asked what a nigger was. He said at least the blacks had made a little progress if an unread, ill-informed tart had not been taught this abusive term. I've got quite a good verbal memory,' she added, half apologetically.

'Evidently.' Ruth's stomach suddenly rumbled extremely loudly. When she grinned, unembarrassed, Browne grinned back. 'Have you eaten since lunch?'

She shook her head. 'It doesn't matter. I realize how important it is to find out who did this awful thing. I'm quite happy to go on.'

'Not till you've had some tea,' Browne decided. 'Caroline here can take you down to the canteen. If you want to go on talking, talk to her.' He suspected that there was much more to tell and that to share it over a meal with one of his minions might seem to Ruth less of a betrayal than to report it here in a formal interview. Besides, if Caroline extracted some useful information, it would give Browne more ammunition for his campaign to get this useful officer transferred to CID.

*

Barry Parker's afternoon kickabout in the park with Paul and Benjie had brought him to a moment of truth. He was not fit. His footwork was still good enough for him to win the ball from Paul, but the lad ended up with possession because Barry couldn't run any further than twenty yards without stopping and panting alarmingly. All the same, he had enjoyed the afternoon's excursion as much as the boys had. He saved face by keeping goal for them until he was breathing easily again.

Paul's enthusiasm waned after he had put about a dozen goals past his father. It wasn't much of a challenge. Barry couldn't decide whether he was being humoured when, after failing to stop several of Benjie's efforts, Paul whispered approvingly, 'You have to let him get some in. He's only little.'

He distracted them with ice cream, and shuddered as they reached with blue fingers for cornets and downed the freezing contents with apparent enjoyment. Barry wrapped his own almost numb hands round his coffee mug as they all sat on the bench outside the refreshment booth, but the heat made them sting and burn. As he rubbed the circulation back into his fingers he was struck by a useful idea.

'Put the ball in the bag now, you two. It's time for some general fitness training. You can do circuits and I'll time you.' He pointed out a route over the muddy grass where he could keep them in sight. Paul, who was developing into a good little athlete, set off.

'Do we just have to run? Paul isn't waiting for me.' Benjie's lower lip began to tremble.

Barry encouraged him. 'It's not a race. I know it's a long way for a little boy to run. You start off while I go in and get some Smarties. You'll get your tube if you run round once. Paul has to go round twice to get his. No cheating, mind!' Barry fished in his pocket for small change as Benjie set off reluctantly.

When he came out of the kiosk, he saw Paul, even though he was ignorant of the reward to come, panting red-faced towards the bench where he had left his jacket. Barry waved him on. 'Round once more, then you can have these.' Paul set off again with a will and Barry settled himself on the bench to admire his former sporting abilities now manifest in his sons. Then he realized that Benjie was not in sight.

Forgetting his lack of fitness, Barry set off at a respectable pace towards the point where the improvised circuit passed nearest to the lake. Thankfully the way was all downhill. Behind a shrub at the bottom of the slope, he found a tearful and breathless Benjie, sitting on the damp grass. He eyed his father dolefully. 'I can't do the uphill bit. My legs aren't long enough.' Once he realized he would not be deprived of his Smarties, his tears dried up, simultaneously with his father's panic.

They walked back to where a triumphant Paul was demolishing his trophy and they all three munched contentedly. 'You'll never guess what I saw.' Benjie, who was developing a nice sense of drama, paused to lick a dribble of chocolate from his chin. 'The vicar and his girlfriend.'

Barry laughed. 'I hope you didn't. He's a married man.'

'I did so.'

Paul gave his young brother a pitying smile. 'Did she have curly brown hair?' Benjie nodded importantly. 'And a light-blue skirt? And a white coat to the bottom of her bum?' Further nods. 'That's his sister. She came to church this morning with Mr Kirkbride's mum. Reuben told us who they were!'

Benjie made sure of the last word by the simple measure of moving out of earshot of his brother before muttering. 'It was his girlfriend so!'

Ruth Roberts's lack of flesh, Caroline observed, was not due to a rigid diet. Nor had the news of the violent death of her friends put her off her food. Both women did justice to the day's special as they talked. Having witnessed quite a number of Browne's urbane and gentle-seeming grillings, Caroline gave her witness a rest and chatted generally, elaborating, not strictly accurately, on a somewhat colourful love life as bait for similar revelations on Ruth's part.

Ruth obliged. 'I was James's student. I stayed on after finals to do a postgrad study on the office of Poet Laureate. Halfway through it I moved in with him – James, I mean, not Ted Hughes – and we began to talk about marriage. I've always got on better with older men. They know themselves, mean what they say. Men mature much later than we do anyway.' She speared a chip and waved it on the end of her fork to emphasize her point.

'The age difference had been totally irrelevant while we just danced, saw films or occasionally went to bed. It all changed as soon as we were living together. Suddenly the whole world felt justified in commenting, especially James's colleagues. Maybe their older wives see me as a threat. They're nice enough on the surface but plenty of folk made sure I heard what was said behind my back.'

'What about your fellow students?'

'They're just as bad. I'm plain and they think I couldn't do any better. It makes me furious. It's an insult to both of us. They think he's past all the things that make life worth living.' She smiled wryly. 'I must admit that if my student friends all come round in a crowd, James finds it exhausting. I get on well with his friends though.'

Caroline, who had eaten at the speed which was usually necessary when she was seconded to a CID enquiry, now placed her knife and fork neatly together and pushed back her plate. 'Your friends, his friends – don't you have common ones?'

Ruth shook her head rather sadly. 'We don't really. I'm a bit afraid that if we do get married we'll become isolated. We don't fit in with couples of either of our generations. In a way, I get an extra kick out of knowing that people disapprove, but that doesn't do away with the problems. When I suggest something, he's always done it, seen it. We can't share many new experiences.'

Caroline nodded and offered coffee, hoping the interruption would not stem the flow of Ruth's confidences.

'How does James see all this?' she asked as she placed the murky liquid apologetically in front of Ruth.

She shook her head ruefully. 'That's what Paula and Marianne got most wrong of all. They envied me because I'm glutted with affection and presents. I try to reassure him that I won't leave him. He even says he could live with an affair. I'm afraid I'll lose respect for him if he denigrates himself any further. He makes desperate little jokes like, "When I'm a hundred and sixteen, you'll be ninety-two". Once he told me that sexual potency might be said to decline increasingly from forty-five but that no one seems to have wondered whether it's because most older men are no longer turned on by their forty-five-plus wives. I hate that expression "turned on".'

Caroline did not feel sanguine about the relationship's future. They sat in companionable silence until Ruth too had finished her food, then she enquired, 'What does your mother think about it?'

Ruth laughed hollowly. 'We talked about it earlier today. She wanted me to wait, think about it longer.'

'What did you say?'

Ruth bit her lip. 'I said, "What, till he's even older?" Still, she's moved from refusing to have him in the house to talking ungraciously about possible wedding arrangements. She'll come round completely with the first grandchild, if we marry and if there is one.'

Caroline grimaced and pushed her coffee away.

'Now it's cold as well as bitter. Did James visit Kingsgate very often?' She watched Ruth's expression become guarded, and knew the girl was well aware that her interrogation proper had begun again.

'Now and then. Occasionally he came to see me, and Paula and Marianne were his students, but he wasn't always in and out. I shouldn't think he was there this weekend.'

'Because you were away?'

'And because of his concert. He's a good and keen violinist and the orchestra's secretary. Anyway, I'm sure your colleague will have asked him about it.'

Caroline decided on a direct appeal. 'Will you tell me whatever you can that could possibly help us find who killed your friends?' She held her hand up to prevent Ruth's protest. 'I know you came here voluntarily and you've been extremely helpful, but I think there's something you're not telling us, possibly to guard someone's reputation. Something to do with your slip-up in telling the DCI that your Nigerian friend called the house in Kingsgate a brothel.' She felt the girl's relief at having her decision made for her.

'Yes, there is. I've only known about it myself for a few days. Jo knew nothing whatever about it. I've known for ages that Marianne and Paula subscribed to one of those lonely hearts magazines. I teased them about it, especially when they'd been offering unwanted advice about James . . .'

'Go on.' Caroline suspected that in his usual flippant fashion, Benny Mitchell had put his finger on the key to the case right at the start of the investigation. The girls had been 'toms' of a kind.

'Well, that's how it started. I seriously warned Paula how dangerous it was . . .'

'Why not both of them?'

'You didn't advise Marianne. She froze you off, and if I'd persevered she wouldn't have taken any notice. Anyway, she soon realized that some of the advertisers were prepared to pay for their sex, and that others wanted to be paid.'

'But that's against—'

'Oh, it wasn't in so many words. She looked for signs, sort of code words. For example, the payers might say "well off" or "generous". Girls offering themselves for sale would put "hard-up student", or "looking for mutually beneficial relationship". After a while, Marianne built up quite a profitable little business out of being a sort of middleman. She rang any local men she thought were offering money and tactfully found out what they were after. Some wanted a link with just one girl, some wanted a collection of them on a rota.'

Caroline sniffed. 'They say variety is the spice of life!'

'After a while, Marianne got extra men on her register because her customers brought friends along.'

'How do you know all this?'

Ruth was now telling her story fluently, no longer in two minds about her revelations being justified. 'Paula said a couple of odd things in conversation one afternoon last week. Something about young men not being what they were looking for. I said something about jobs and she said that if they were earning they wouldn't be advertising, so then I knew they were being paid. It was confirmed when I realized how angry Marianne was. I got Paula on her own later on and asked her what she'd got herself into. She half wanted to tell me, to enlist my help to get free of it, but half of her was still enjoying the sex and the secrecy. She was certainly terrified of Marianne finding out how much she'd told me. I worked out quite a lot without Paula realizing how much she'd given away. She wasn't very bright.'

'I don't see why anyone should go through Marianne rather than just using the magazine. How did it work?'

'I didn't find out all the details. I don't think Paula did either. The girls were given cash each time they met a man and Marianne was given a monthly cheque for keeping each man's name on her register and making sure that a girl was instantly available whenever he could snatch an hour away from family and responsibilities. Her virtue – not quite the right word, perhaps – for the men was that all her girls were fairly local. They don't have much time that doesn't need to be accounted for and none of it was wasted in travelling. Paula said some of them didn't give their real names, just a first name that was false so that prattlers didn't let the real ones drop in conversation. Well, she should have known about that. That's really all I know.'

Her expression changed suddenly, so that Caroline asked, 'What's the matter?'

'Well, unlike Jo, I really am a fairly impoverished

student. I'm not ready to move back in with James and I don't suppose I can have my room in Kingsgate yet – if ever. It'll depend on who the house has been left to. I could manage a hotel room if it's really necessary but not for long. Could you find out for me what the situation is? By the way, I draw the line at a police cell.'

As Mitchell brought James Enright into the station foyer to wait until Ruth was ready to leave, Magic Powers waved the telephone receiver at him. 'Your wife.'

Mitchell was alarmed. Ginny rang him at work only in the direst emergency. He grabbed the receiver unceremoniously from Magic. 'What's wrong?'

She sounded calm enough. 'Nothing. Just don't come home tonight.'

'What?'

'Go to the pub if you finish early. Don't get in till at least half past ten.'

Mitchell blinked. 'Would you mind saying that again?'

Virginia chuckled. 'Not likely. You might claim I've given you permission to do it twice!'

'What the . . .' but she was no longer there. Pity. He'd been going to tell her that if he was drinking under orders the cost would have to come out of her housekeeping money!

Chapter Ten

Having given Sergeant Taylor an hour to repent of her sins, Browne now summoned her. She stood just inside his doorway, facing him and obviously about to speak. He waved a hand to silence her and ushered her to his visitor's chair. If he let her offer an apology, he would have to accept it with no more said and the constraint between her and the rest of the team would remain unexplained and unresolved.

In personal affairs, plain speaking was the only way he knew, and he had worked with this girl long enough for their relationship to be more than just professional. He addressed her hard profile, ignoring her pique at not being allowed to speak. 'I don't want to listen to you grovel, Jennifer. I want to get things sorted out. You've never struck me as the type to suffer from the daftest kind of women's lib nonsense. I expect you've got problems both personal and domestic in dealing with Paul's death. We want to help, not to humour you but to make things as easy as we can. But we don't have psychic powers. If we get it wrong, let us know. But please do it in so many words, not with snide comments in briefings or by biting the heads off former colleagues who are trying to welcome you.'

For some seconds she sat, looking down, hands still in her lap. Then she raised her eyes to his face and gave him her old grin. 'I think what I want is a good talk with Ginny. In fact, I rang up this afternoon to fix it.'

Browne laughed and dismissed her by taking a folder from his top drawer and opening it on the desk. 'That will either kill or cure. If you survive, I'll see you in the morning.'

Virginia was watching through the front window as the red Fiesta pulled up outside, and had her front door open before her visitor reached it. The strident bell had more than once wakened both babies. She kept Jennifer standing just inside her hallway and gave her a lengthy appraisal, trying to pinpoint the changes in her.

The heavy dark hair was no longer drawn back from the oval face into a knot at the nape, in a manner that had formerly made her look like an Andrea del Sarto madonna. Now it was cropped at ear level with a spiky fringe that reached her slightly thinned brows. Where there had been curves there were now angles, though she still moved like a ballerina. The flowing skirts she had associated with the old Jennie had been replaced by expensively tailored trousers. Virginia had the impression that Jennifer had attempted to look less feminine, but, in spite of all her efforts, she had succeeded only in looking more so.

Jennifer waited for the inspection to be over, then asked, 'Will I do?'

'Very nice.' Virginia grinned, and led the way to the sitting room. 'I hope you're not in a baby-worshipping mood. I've only just got them off.' She dropped into a sagging but comfortable armchair and waved Jennifer to its twin. 'You'll be thankful not to smell my appalling coffee being brewed. We'll drink Australian plonk whilst we bare our souls, and tea whilst we sober up.' She filled two glasses and pushed one across the coffee table.

'You can go first. There isn't time for polite preliminaries. The twins are very restless babies and I've told Benny he can come home at half past ten, so you'll have to get on with it.'

Jennifer chuckled. 'Benny's mellowed a bit. You're exactly the same.'

Virginia shrugged and decided to risk switching off the baby alarm. The distracting little snuffling noises ceased, then she wondered whether the almost complete silence that followed would be harder for Jennifer to break. She broke it herself. 'Benny's thirty-three. I'm only twenty-four. I can mellow later on.' She did a rapid calculation. Jennifer must be just thirty. Plenty of time to pick up the pieces and begin again. 'I can understand that you're still missing Paul, and that two little girls don't make it easy to get back to working in what basically is still a man's world, but I don't understand the problem here in Cloughton. You're accepted on equal terms, valued for what you do, respected for what you contributed when you worked here before.'

'You don't understand anything. I'm not missing Paul at all.'

Virginia stared. Jennifer put her empty glass down on the table. Virginia decided the gesture was not a hint. Her visitor was an abstemious drinker, unless she had changed in this respect too since last time they had met. If they were to have the talk that Jennifer had asked for, it would be as well to delay a refill.

Suddenly she began to speak. 'Being married to Paul was like having a depressive illness. Even after just a few weeks he began to hang over me like a dark cloud, trying to make me into something I wasn't, making me feel guilty for everything that, instinctively, I wanted.'

'I don't understand. I always thought of you as a fighter. Why didn't you stand up to him?'

'Because what I was fighting was so insubstantial. If he'd hit me, I'd have either retaliated or left him. If he'd ordered me to do things, I could have refused. If he'd forbidden me, I could have defied him and done whatever it was. What I couldn't cope with was his intangible disapproval. I could have lived with making him angry but he didn't get angry, only offended and hurt.'

'Yes, I know the type. So why did you marry him? Was he different in the beginning, when you first met him?'

Jennifer shook her head. 'No, that type can't

change. Oh, Ginny, I *fancied* him. You have to admit he was everyone's idea of a beautiful man.'

Virginia chuckled. 'I suppose so, compared with Benny.' Jennifer joined in with a semi-hysterical giggle as both women considered the physical attributes of fourteen-stone Mitchell, with his army-style haircut, square muscular frame and belligerent cast of features. 'Tell me about your leaving Cloughton.'

Jennifer nodded. 'In one way, I was glad to go. Paul was pleased he was being promoted and I'd grown to hate working part-time. I was only given short-term things to do and I was never in charge of a section of an enquiry because, half the time, I wasn't there to report back to. At home, I was constantly apologizing to Paul, and mentally to Lucy, for not being there for them in the way that Paul expected. It was totally unsatisfactory.

'I don't know whether my getting pregnant again was Paul's way of imprisoning me or my own capitulation to what he wanted.' Her tone was bitter. 'And all the time, I had to watch Benny making things easy for you to carry on studying, at the expense of his own career.'

'Yes. I nearly divorced him for it!'

Jennifer sat up. 'Are you serious?'

Virginia shook back her long black frizz of curls that badly needed expert attention. 'I'll answer that another time. Just carry on.'

'Well, whichever it was, it didn't work. Once the new house was bought and organized I was even more dissatisfied. Neither of us faced the problems. We quarrelled about other things, stupid things.'

'Like?'

'Like names for the baby. Paul was certain it would be another girl and suggested Hannah and Charlotte and Alice! Just like Lucy and Jane that he'd insisted on first time round, cosy, old-fashioned names always in favour in the middle classes. He said he loved my name and all its domestic associations, Jenny Wren! Spinning Jenny! I vowed never to answer to Jennie again. When I took a temporary post at Paul's station, I introduced myself as Jennifer and that's how I was known.'

'What did Paul think about this temporary post?' Now that her guest's tale was satisfactorily unfolding, Virginia leaned across to fill her glass.

'He was all for it at first. It was a maternity leave, so there was a definite final date and he thought his bosses would be grateful to him for "lending" me!' Jennifer drank half the contents of her glass angrily and banged it down. 'I'd become deceitful by then, and booked myself on a course that began just before the mat. leave ended.'

'That's how you're Holmes trained?'

'Yes, and it immediately made me much more employable. With that card up my sleeve I became more determined. Paul's mum was on my side once she sensed rebellion was afoot. She told Paul my talents were being wasted and that she would cheerfully mind her grandchildren.'

'That was useful.'

'In a way, but I resented her at first. I wanted to take on the whole world and fight alone, not accept support from a member of the enemy camp. Without her now, nothing would be possible.' Jennifer seemed surprised to find her glass empty and placed it, quietly this time, on the table.

Virginia topped it up again. 'Bring that with you and we'll raid the kitchen.' She grinned as her guest tried to look enthusiastic. She was a mother confessor, not a cordon-bleu cook. Jennifer would have to make do with the best she could provide.

'So, I see why you want to be Jennifer. How did you settle on Judith?'

Jennifer chuckled. 'I picked up a copy of the Apocrypha in a junk shop, just out of idle curiosity, and I read about what she did to Holofernes. When I suggested it to Paul, minus the reason for my choice, he said it was a nice comfortable name. After that, names were not the main cause of contention. Shall I brew this tea? The kettle's boiling.'

Virginia took her head out of the fridge and nodded. When they were seated at the kitchen table she asked, 'Paul was killed in a car accident, wasn't he? Was it a chase?'

Jennifer, munching valiantly, shook her head. 'He was attending an RTA. There was quite a nasty pile-up on a wet night. A young girl was involved, a chemist who worked for a drugs firm that experimented on animals. She wasn't hurt and her car wasn't much damaged but she was shocked. Paul offered to drive her home in her own vehicle. A bomb, that had failed to go off even when the car was hit in the accident, detonated when they started it up again. It killed them both. The girl was supposed to check her vehicle whenever she got into it but I suppose you get careless.'

Jennifer reached over to fill her own glass and this time sipped slowly from it, gathering courage from it for her next revelation. 'Paul died on the very day I'd finally decided to issue an ultimatum about my career. I'd cooked a special meal, hoping for Lucy's sake that things wouldn't get too acrimonious, but I knew I was ending my marriage. Paul would never have allowed me to set conditions.

'I can remember every detail of that day. I got up with my decision made. As I was making the early tea, the sky through the kitchen window was a mackerel pattern, red on navy, and I remembered my mother always saying, "A red sky in the morning, shepherd's warning." I was glad of the wild weather. It fitted my mood and kept my anger stoked up. And then he never came home. And, instead of being sorry, I was furious with him because he'd cheated me out of asserting myself and getting back my self-respect. That's the chief reason I'm sorry he's dead and I feel so guilty.' Suddenly, she was sobbing, her face hidden in her hands.

Virginia put a hand on Jennifer's shoulder. When it was shaken off, she calmly went on drinking her tea. After a minute or two, when Jennifer took out a man's handkerchief to dry her eyes, she continued the conversation as though there had been no interruption. 'So now you want to make your stand against somebody else. Otherwise, you won't feel you've put his domination behind you. And you've picked Benny.'

Jennifer looked surprised. 'I suppose I have. I'm sorry.'

'Well, Benny's a good choice. His back's broad enough. Get it out of your system soon though. It must be holding up your life just as much as Paul ever did.'

Babasola Ogunade enjoyed running, especially in the dark. Even as he covered his first mile, he felt pleasure in the control he held over his well-muscled body. After a few more, he knew he would feel a lessening of the impatience, sometimes anger, that built up in him as the academic limitations of his teachers hampered his studies, and the fecklessness of his juvenile delinquent associates limited the amount of money he could acquire.

Tonight he wished he could run for twenty or thirty miles. It was mild for January, and the air was damp so that he could breathe through his mouth without his throat becoming dry and irritated. His new running shoes crunched on the cinder track through the allotments which had not protected them from becoming sodden and clay-smeared. Still, if they wouldn't clean up properly, there were plenty more where those had come from.

He reached the gate at the far end of the allotments, passed through and jogged to a clump of bushes by the path that led on into the council estate. Doubling back, he swore softly as he heard the laden youths puffing and panting as they came towards him. It was a wonder that half the occupants of the houses that overlooked the path had not come out to see what was going on.

He relieved Cracker of some of his load, which was the heavier, and hissed angrily at them both. 'For God's sake, get yourselves into shape. If you don't stop shooting that filthy stuff, you're going to snuff it even before the pay-out.'

Dez's voice was sulky. 'If I could kick it I wouldn't be having owt to do with you!'

'Why did you leave the van without waiting for my signal?'

Cracker looked puzzled. 'We heard you whistle.'

'I wouldn't be stupid enough to whistle . . .' He looked about him, tense now. 'Where did the whistle come from?'

'From my direction, I think.' The voice came from behind the flashlight which was suddenly dazzling them and which, for them, illuminated only its owner's black and white chequered hatband. The constable ran his light over Sola from head to foot. 'Nice gear. Two sports shops have been done over in the last month. Didn't you find all you needed in the first one?'

On Monday morning, Sergeant Taylor flicked a comb about her head which was all her new haircut needed to make it presentable, despite the rain she had dashed through, hatless, to reach the station foyer. She examined the face that looked back at her from the cloakroom mirror. She was not a Jennie any longer. A change of heart, followed by a change of name, was very biblical. What was good enough for Abraham and St Paul would do for her.

She set off for Browne's office and met Mitchell at the foot of the stairs. He regarded her with mock solicitude. 'You survived last night, then?'

She grinned. 'The pep talk or the sausage rolls?'

'Neither seems to have done you any harm.'

She followed him up the stairs, her feet having to find the steps from long use, since his back - broad, as his wife had observed - blocked out most of the light from the staircase window. She allowed him to open the door for her and they joined the officers already assembled, only just in time for Browne's eight o'clock deadline.

The DCI called them to order and quickly summarized the previous day's findings, inviting the officers concerned in each aspect of the enquiry to contribute their personal observations. Neither Mitchell nor Jennifer chose to take advantage of this opportunity. Jennifer's discovery that the girls' handbags were missing had been eclipsed by their having been found in the allotment shed. Mitchell's visit to the vicarage, in search of background information on Cavill Jackson had, he considered, been a complete waste of time. He had found himself taking tea with the two Mrs Kirkbrides as he awaited the return of the vicar and his sister. When the walkers had eventually arrived back, Evensong had been imminent and the talk with Tony Kirkbride had been put off till later this morning.

Browne passed on the information gathered from the house-to-house enquiries which had for once been quite productive. 'A Mrs Johnson from number one saw Jo Merry backing her car out on to the road just after four. Jo had told her that a friend was taking his car off the road for the next three months. She had agreed to have it at the back of her garage for the rest of the winter. She'd be putting hers back when his was stowed away . . .'

Several voices spoke at once.

'So that's how the other three bodies came in. He'd only need a cover over them in the car. There's a door leading directly to the hall from the garage . . .'

'He must have killed her as soon as he arrived, before she had a chance to put her car away . . .'

'So now we're at least sure it's a man . . .'

Browne called his meeting to order again. 'The chap from number four was walking his dog on the grass opposite. He reckons he saw a series of flashes through gaps in the curtains, "like a Morse-code message", he says.'

'Photographs!' They all looked at Mitchell. 'We'd better start looking for them. And we'd better look for someone with the experience and the equipment to develop his own. He wouldn't risk having those pictures processed commercially. Didn't one or two American multi-killers take photographs of their victims . . .?'

Browne nodded. 'We'll bear that in mind. Yes, Andy?'

'We were on the knocker round the allotments last

night.' DC Craig indicated himself and Winters. 'Several people reported seeing a young black chap hanging about. He usually had a couple of white youths with him. It was thought he was taking over the vacant plot till Sam Cooper saw Benson digging yesterday.'

'Ruth Roberts was telling me . . .' Browne looked at Caroline Webster, who had coloured and stuttered into silence. 'Forget it, sir. Considering the number of non-whites living in Cloughton it's not likely he's the same man.' Sola, whoever he was, had a right to be on the lookout for prejudice against his colour. Having aroused everyone's curiosity, however, she was obliged to give them Ruth's account of his altercation with Jo Merry and his acquaintance with the other victims.

Browne rescued her with his continuation of the story. 'Sam Cooper's friend, Tommy, who had to give up his allotment, is the father of one of the youths we picked up last night. He thought his dad's shed would make a convenient repository for a few TVs, video machines and so on.'

'And the four handbags?'

Browne shook his head at Winters. 'No, Chris. They all purport to know nothing of the handbags. Mr Ogunade claims he was merely on a training run for some university cross-country event. He says he turned back when he heard the puffing and panting behind him. He knows the boys by sight and thought one of them might be having an asthma attack. The lads, of course, claim they only did the burglaries because Ogunade threatened them. Ogunade points out that he's clean, whilst both lads have records of petty thefts going back to their time in the womb. At the moment, we don't really care either way about the electrical goods but the three of them will remain our guests until we've sorted out their connection with those handbags—'

He was interrupted by his telephone and the whole team listened as he picked up the receiver. The desk sergeants all knew better than to interrupt a briefing for something unimportant. They learned little from Browne's monosyllabic replies. When the call was finished, he caught Jennifer's eye. 'The couple who live at number eleven Kingsgate were looking after their grandson for the afternoon on Saturday. He played on the grass across the road, kicking a ball. He's downstairs with his mother.'

Mitchell winked at Jennifer. 'Let's hope he's nosy.'

Jennifer ran down the stairs to the foyer, pausing to look over the banister as she reached the last flight. Mother and son sat together on the hideous orange plastic padded seats under the window. She decided to talk to them there. It would be more comfortable and less intimidating than an interview room.

Not that the boy looked likely to be intimidated. He was observing the comings and goings in the foyer with a lively interest, whilst his mother tried to slick down his unruly hair. Jennifer suspected that the child had brought his mother along, rather than the reverse.

Magic Powers came over from the desk. 'DS Taylor, Mrs Appleby and Ryan.' Somehow he managed to make this economical introduction sound quite friendly.

The bench seat formed a half-circle so that Jennifer

could sit next to the mother and face the child. She had the impression that Mrs Appleby was relieved and Ryan disappointed to be interviewed by a female. She addressed the child. 'I'd guess you were about nine, Ryan.'

'He's not quite eight.'

Ryan gave his mother a reproachful glance, but seemed pleased, as Jennifer had meant him to be, at this flattering estimate of his maturity. 'I've got some information for you.'

'So I hear. We shall be very glad of it.'

'I've written it down.' He fished in his pocket for a small notebook. 'Will you type it out so that I can sign it?'

Jennifer was amused. 'You seem to know all about how we work.'

'He won't have to appear in court, will he?' Mrs Appleby raised imploring eyes, as, with a different plea, did her son. 'It might be my duty to,' he told his mother hopefully, not taking his eyes from Jennifer's face.

She assumed a serious expression. 'May I read your statement?'

Ryan was deprecating now. 'It's not a statement exactly. It's a list of car numbers. I wrote a list of the numbers of all the cars that went along Kingsgate on Saturday from after dinner till it began to get dark and Gran made me go indoors. I like making lists.'

'You couldn't,' Jennifer told him with perfect truth, 'have brought us anything more helpful. Would you be willing to lend us your notebook?' He seemed reluctant and she added hastily, 'Or shall I go and photocopy the pages we'll need?'

He beamed. 'Can I work the copier?'

Jennifer considered. 'If you only do exactly what I tell you.' He followed her happily to a small office behind the desk and, preoccupied with jabbing his finger at the appropriate buttons, chattered cheerfully on the topics Jennifer introduced. 'Did any cars go past too quickly for you to see the number?'

He shook his head. 'Kingsgate isn't on the way to anywhere, so most of the cars were slowing down to park. There was one with the number plate too muddy to read. I made up a pretend that there was a robber in it who'd muddied them on purpose.'

'Did the robber get away?'

'No, he drove into the garage of one of the houses.'

'Can you remember which one?'

He stopped jabbing to consider. 'I'm not sure which number it was but I could show you the drive. It was one of those that leads to two houses. Can I make an extra copy for me?'

Jennifer nodded. 'We can copy some of the other pages as well, if you like. Did you put the muddy car down on your list?'

He gave her a scornful glance. 'I couldn't, could I? But I noted down the time instead. It was eleven minutes past four, just as Gran was calling me in. I might have been able to see the numbers better if it hadn't been starting to get dark, I suppose.'

Jennifer collected up the copies they had made

and fished a packet from her pocket. 'Do you like humbugs?'

He sought a polite version of the truth. 'They aren't my really, really favourite.'

Jennifer fished again. 'What about chocolate?' He accepted this and thanked her. 'Did you notice what kind of car it was that was muddy and went into the garage?'

'I'm not sure. Is it important?' When Jennifer nodded, he put on the agonized expression children always assume to convince adults that they are doing their best to produce a required answer. 'I'm afraid I don't know the make but it was old, the sort that people don't buy any more. It was fairly big and dark red under the mud – or it might have been brown. Oh! and it was an estate car like Mr St Clair's and I think the back seat was folded down.'

'Well done. What about the driver?'

'It was a man with a fur hat on and a big scarf.' He pulled out a clean handkerchief. 'I'll clean my mouth and my fingers if we've finished eating chocolate.'

Jennifer bit her lip, knowing she would probably forget to replace her daughters' weekly treat, and gave him the rest of the bar, silently apologizing to them. 'Did you see anything else that would have made a good pretend?'

Ryan shook his head. 'Not in the front street. There was a boy in a tree at the back, a big boy, a bit old for climbing trees. I could see him when I was dribbling my ball round the benches at the edge of the grass. He was spying on everyone.'

Chapter Eleven

Jennifer escorted the Appleby family to their car. Now she had better go back to Browne's office for further instructions. On the first small landing, she met Mitchell coming down. 'Vicarage,' he announced in answer to her tacit enquiry. 'Then to see Rory Jackson. He's Cavill's brother, but I'll be glad to ask him a few questions as Jonathan Parker's probation officer. The DCI's going to find out from Jo Merry's solicitor who gets the loot.'

'What about me?'

Mitchell shrugged. 'No idea, but if you're finished by half twelve I'll buy you lunch in the Fleece.'

'Why?' She grinned to take the sting out of this rather ungracious response.

'Because it's my turn after yesterday, or as your reward for disposing of Ginny's sausage rolls, whichever reason you're happiest with.'

Jennifer made an effort. 'I'm very happy just to be treated to lunch. Thank you.' She completed her climb to Browne's office and presented him with her photocopied lists. She expected to be given her action sheet and was surprised and dismayed when Browne waved her to a seat. Surely he didn't expect a potted version of her conversation with his daughter? She'd had her reprimand, and he would have had his apology if he hadn't put her off before she got it out.

When he spoke again, she offered him a silent one. 'Where, if anywhere, do you think Jon Parker fits into this case?'

She replied only after some moments' reflection. 'I'd have said nowhere at all until I spoke to that child just now. I can't justify it, but as soon as he mentioned a boy in a tree the Parker youth sprang to mind. It could of course have been anyone with the agility to get up there.'

'We did promise his mother that we'd make enquiries about him. Perhaps, until some reports come in that really help us with the murder enquiry, you wouldn't mind seeing Barry Parker's second family. Just poke and prod a bit, see what you can turn up. Particularly see if you can get Stephanie's version of her brother's attack on her.'

Jennifer had her own reasons for being pleased with her assignment. She had reached the door when Browne turned back to the papers in his hand. 'Just a minute. Since in your temporary absence from Cloughton you've become a computer whizz, you could go and do your stuff with these car numbers before you leave.'

She tossed her head. 'I think I was quite sufficiently computer-literate to perform that simple task when I last worked for you.' She collected coffee in a polystyrene cup, taking it, against all regulations, into the computer room. Ryan's list was extensive and she feared she was in for a long and tedious session.

She was not mistaken, but the results of her patient search pleased her. She noted her success in her pocketbook, then checked over the main points of her chat with Ryan. There was a further question for Mrs Appleby. As she identified herself, the voice on the other end of the line cooled perceptibly. Jennifer reassured her. 'I've quite finished with your son and I'm grateful to him. This is a question for you. Have you any friends or neighbours called Sinclair?'

'Colin St Clair lives opposite us at number twenty-two.' The information was given grudgingly.

'Could you, by any chance, tell me what kind of car he drives?'

Now the woman's voice was smiling. 'I should be able to. You hear a eulogy of it if you even say good morning to him and I'm surprised he hasn't polished it away. It's a 1986 BMW 325 estate. You're not telling me . . .?'

'No, I have no reason to connect him with the case but Ryan saw a similar car on Saturday. Now we know what kind to look for.' Jennifer replaced the receiver and looked at her watch. There wasn't much point now in trying to see any of the new Parker family before lunch. According to Magic, Browne had not returned from his visit to Jo Merry's solicitor. How should she keep herself busy till he did?

She fetched more coffee from the dispenser in the corridor, pulled a couple of sheets of paper from the printer she had been using and headed four columns with the murdered girls' names. She bore these and her coffee to the table in the incident room where the case files lay. Laboriously, she turned over sheets of reports and filled her columns.

She found Marianne Baxter by far the most interesting of the four girls. Motherless since the age of eight, she had helped her father care for her sister, who was six years younger. The father had become ill when she was fifteen and wheelchair-bound a year later, since when the progress of his disease seemed to have slowed. Now, with help from the social services, he was cared for by the younger sister, eighteen years old and far less academic than Marianne. When she had got her degree in the summer, Marianne was to have returned home to Carlisle to find work in the town whilst Melanie, in her turn, found some training that would qualify her for a career. Meanwhile, she sent home generous gifts of money, saved, not from a student grant, as her credulous family believed, but from her takings as a pimp.

Jennifer added questions to the list of facts. Was there any paperwork from Marianne's scam, and, if so, who had it now? Even though they thought she had 'a little evening job, bar work, I think', did Marianne's father, reported to be in full possession of his mental faculties, really believe that it allowed her to provide for them so liberally? And what had been going on inside the girl's head? How could the same girl turn her landlady's house into a knocking shop and then put the best part of the money it earned her into an envelope each month and send it to her dutiful sister and crippled father?

Paula and Briony seemed only one-dimensional by comparison, vain, shallow, greedy – though, in a way, Jennifer felt sorry for both of them. Briony had been three months pregnant and chiefly concerned with the question of which possible father would prove the most generous, but her own parents seemed to have been equally feckless and had probably taught her no better. According to the filed reports, her parents knew neither which course she was supposed to be studying nor where she stayed when she came to college each term. Her course had actually been the same as Paula's but she had not been assigned James Enright as her English tutor. Jennifer scribbled a final question in her column. Could Barry, encumbered with several children already and disinclined to own to another one, be the father of Jonathan Parker?

Paula's parents seemed different. They had been bursting with pride in their daughter's academic career and desperately anxious for her to succeed. What a pity that they hadn't known her better, had more realistic expectations for her, been satisfied with her as she was. Then she might be still alive and safely employed in some useful but undemanding work that provided her with a legitimate income.

Jennifer contemplated the final empty column and wondered if she were merely playing a time-wasting game. Giving herself the benefit of the doubt, she began filling in Jo Merry's details, a mother lost to the records after five years' neglect, eleven years in a children's home, part-time work to keep her alive until she finally got a break that made up for it all – or did it? And somehow, all the members of this disparate group had managed to make one man murderously angry. At least, Jennifer sincerely hoped it was only one man. And, as far as any of the team could discover, only Marianne's little scheme linked them all.

If the one man was insane, of course, then maybe even this link was irrelevant. Jennifer drank the cold dregs of her coffee and looked forward to her lunch.

As the vicarage door opened in answer to his ring, Mitchell was relieved to see no sign of Mrs Kirkbride. The vicar himself received him. Obviously primed by his wife, he escorted his visitor to his study, settled him in a chair and began without preamble. 'You want to talk to me about Cavill. I should have thought his brother would be more use to you – or have you come here because you require a spiritual assessment?' He raised an ironic eyebrow.

Mitchell sat back, taking stock of his surroundings. Jean Kirkbride had told him the previous day that they had resisted the church commissioners' attempts to rehouse them in a smaller, more easily maintained vicarage. Tony provided out of his own means for the comfort, warmth and convenience that the house offered. Not that there was luxury or ostentation. The man's clothes matched his house in that they were of good quality and comfortable but low-key. The thick, plum-coloured cotton sweatshirt and worn and faded jeans were practical and flattering.

'I came here,' Mitchell told him, 'because he called you his mentor, his substitute father. He didn't mention his brother, though we are aware that there is one.'

Kirkbride had seated himself in the chair opposite Mitchell. 'That's hard on Rory. Their father died in a factory accident when he had just left school and Cavill was quite small, but their mother seems to have given them all the security they needed and the three of them are still very close. He did confide in me too, of course. Possibly he said more about his relationship with Jo Merry to me than to Rory, though it was little enough.'

'Now she's dead, can you tell me how you saw it?'

Kirkbride smiled. 'Yes, I'm willing to do that. I'm sure it won't incriminate him. She intrigued him. He helped her but he wasn't really involved with her emotionally. He doesn't seem greatly affected by her death in itself, though he's horrified, of course, by the manner of it.' He stopped speaking and they were both comfortable with the silence.

Mitchell used it to make an assessment of his witness. The pepper-and-salt hair that had recently been auburn was thick and crinkled; the eyes, blue and intelligent, were deeply set and the rest of his features regular. The man had on him that sheen that came from good living and freedom from financial worries, yet his face was lined and weathered. His money, Mitchell thought approvingly, had not been used to protect him from unpleasant experience. His profession would have seen to that.

Kirkbride began to speak again. 'Men can never be put into neat pigeon-holes, and hence nor can criminals. You've come to ask me if I think Cavill could be one and I have to reply that I don't know. That's not to say that I have any reason to doubt or suspect him. The longer I serve as a minister of the Church, the more I realize that I know almost nothing of human nature.

'What I can see clearly is that music is part of Cavill's essential nature – a very large part.' He looked up at Mitchell and grinned. 'Ordinary people like you and me don't have talents. They have delusions about things they can do that give them confidence to perform in that area. Cavill, though, has a real gift. I think he could be capable of attacking anyone who was threatening to stifle that vital part of him.'

'Do you think Jo Merry was threatening him?'

'No, but I'm not sure whether Cavill doesn't think she was.'

'You're saying he might have killed her if she'd tried to make him spend more time with her and less with his organ and his choir?'

Kirkbride shook his lion head. 'It isn't so simple. He's a musician. Music is what he lives for. But he's also a man, rather a nice bloke. You should see him with the choirboys – and the older choristers too. He doesn't use them or exploit them. He cares about them, tries to share with them this thing that for him is the meaning of life. There's no conflict there, of course.

He only picks the people who want, and have the ability, to share it with him.'

'Was Jo musical?'

He shook his head. 'Not as Cavill defined it, though she did take an intellectual interest in all kinds of cultural activities. Because he's kind-hearted, Cavill wanted to make up to her for the bloody awful life she'd had, give her pleasure by taking her into his musical circle. What he couldn't do was come out of the musical aura that separates him from most of the rest of mankind and meet her on her own level.

'Just once, quite recently, he came and tried to talk to me about it, but conversations are shallow. People run away from each other and hide their vulnerable selves behind screens of banality or politeness or wit. All he managed actually to say was, "I'm worried that Jo's getting too fond of me." He was afraid that she wanted first place in his life – and that was something he had to save for his music.'

For another half-hour the detective sergeant and the Anglican minister sat together, consuming excellent home-made biscuits and even better coffee. When he got up to go the sergeant was unhappy. Until this morning Mitchell had been fairly certain that crimes such as he was investigating would have been impossibly out of character for a man as likeable as Cavill Jackson. Now he felt he had been shown a set of circumstances in which he might have been driven to them.

*

Jennifer arrived at the Fleece just three minutes after Mitchell's deadline. She found him looking bewildered, holding the regular menu in his hand whilst he ran his eyes over the dishes of the day chalked in a list on the board on the opposite wall. He grinned as she slipped into the seat beside him. 'I preferred this place when I first used to come. There were two dishes to choose from and three at the weekend. Now, by the time you've read to the end of what's available, you've forgotten the beginning.'

Jennifer nodded. 'And, whatever you choose, you don't enjoy it properly because all the time you're wondering if one of the alternatives might have been better.'

'Why don't you close your eyes and stab?'

'It might come up caviar and fillet steak.'

'So? I haven't given *you* a price limit.'

She pulled a face at him. 'Then you should have. You've got four kids to keep. Ploughman's, I think. The rest's too rich and fancy when you need to keep your wits about you.'

In the Fleece, the police were known and usually served quickly. Mitchell described his trip to the vicarage as he emptied his first glass and attacked a meal of salad, cheese and pork pie more substantial and elaborate than any ploughman would have carried to his field. It was difficult to summarize what the vicar had said, consisting as it did of impression and opinion rather than a recital of facts.

'I'm not sure whether what I got was useful or not. I had the impression that Kirkbride was trying to convince himself as well as me that his organist was innocently caught up in all this business. I ended up with this picture of a genius, inconvenienced by the appetites of a normal bloke. Just the sort to need a tom now and again, but having to keep it quiet because of the church choir and because of the people who invite him to play in cathedrals all over the place. A reputation as a bit of a rake wouldn't matter if he played something like a fiddle that he could carry around with him, but most organs are in churches so he'd have to keep his nose clean.' Mitchell chewed gloomily as Jennifer got up to replenish their glasses.

Another pint seemed to cheer him up. 'At least Kirkbride did talk about Jackson, so this morning wasn't the complete waste of time that yesterday was.'

'I gather you were a captive audience for a compulsive talker.'

Mitchell was defensive. 'Well, she kept insisting that he'd be back any minute. She went on and on telling me how much he needed the hour's break and exercise, as though she had to defend him for not being there when I wanted to see him. Either that, or she thought it was her husband's alibi I'd come to get. She took me through his whole crowded weekend from Friday night when he was seeing to an old chap who's pretending to be senile, through umpteen hospital visits on Saturday and a blow-by-blow account of his sermon preparation that Jackson interrupted after we'd let him go on Saturday night.

'She seemed to think Cavill's visit at that hour a bit of an imposition. She didn't think much of Kirkbride's going out with his sister either. I tried everything to get her to keep on the subject of Jackson even if it was a long grumble, but then she went haring off on their life history as vicar and housekeeper in Crewe, then Maidstone, then Truro . . .'

'Then what?'

'Then I stopped listening, till she came full circle. They ended up back where they'd started in Cloughton so as to give the sister a hand with the old lady. Not that she seemed to need a lot of help. Sharp enough, though she has trouble getting about. What about you?'

'You needn't order me a Zimmer yet.' He gave her a long-suffering smile. 'I was supposed to be seeing Stephanie Parker but I got diverted on to the car numbers the Appleby child gave us. Enright was there on Saturday afternoon.'

'The little nun's bloke?'

'I wouldn't call living over the brush with a man twice her age very nunlike.'

'No, I suppose not. It's just the doe eyes and the flat hair.'

'I'm not sure we've given her enough attention. She seems to be the only person, except presumably a solicitor somewhere, who knew how much Jo Merry was worth. She says she heard about the murders on the radio on Sunday morning but didn't come back till the evening because her mother needed her, and she had nothing to tell us that was urgent. More likely she needed time to decide how much we needed to know and how much could be decently veiled.'

'How long would it have taken her to nip back from Nottingham?'

'But why should she?' Jennifer liked watching Mitchell chase hares. Often they led him to a new aspect of the case and if not, he usually accepted it with reasonable grace.

'What if she was involved in Marianne's racket too? It would have to be on the management side. She hasn't got what a tom needs.' Jennifer thought that would depend on the customer but she did not interrupt Mitchell's flow of speculations. 'Maybe she wasn't happy with her share of the profits.'

'Maybe,' Jennifer interrupted, half serious now, 'they threatened to tell Enright about it if she didn't keep in line.'

'What if he'd found out anyway, and *he* did it to get her out of it all?'

'It might be worth someone seeing her again,' Jennifer agreed, 'and someone will definitely have to talk to Enright.'

'What if,' Mitchell demanded excitedly, 'Jo's left the house to her? She was the one who knew where everything came from . . .' He realized Jennifer was no longer listening but staring at something behind him. 'What are you thinking?'

'That I don't think Ruth's a serious contender, and I was wondering . . .'

'Yes?'

'Whether you can afford to buy us some almond tart.'

'That and coffee as well, on condition that you

don't shoot me down when I ask the DCI to check Ruth Roberts through her weekend.'

Jennifer shook her head. 'It's a pity she had to go away. The frustrating thing is that what the girls did over the two days, where they went, who they talked to and so on, they only talked about to each other. Only in the case of Briony Cocker is there someone who was around when she was called away. I'd like to follow that up, talk to the folk she was staying with, get every single detail out of them.'

Feeling that this reflected badly on what Mitchell had obtained from the Staniforths, she added hastily, 'When you saw them, she was only a naughty girl who had played truant from her friend's wedding and might just have found herself an interesting date.'

Reluctantly, they left the warm fug of the pub and walked briskly through the chill drizzle towards the police station some five hundred yards away. Halfway along the row of shops, Mitchell stopped to allow an elderly woman to cross the pavement in front of him. She bore a large plastic bag of washing and disappeared into Washing World.

'Just a minute.' He almost sprinted the rest of the way to the station, cutting across the car park to his vehicle with Jennifer in mystified pursuit. He loaded her with two large and brightly coloured car rugs whilst he locked the boot. 'Can you work those complicated coin-operated dry-cleaning machines? In the launderette!'

'Yes. Why?'

Having paused to retrieve his property, Mitchell

had set off back towards the shops. 'Have you got that inquisition for Briony's hostess on the tip of your tongue?'

Jennifer grinned and nodded. 'Is she in there? How long have we got?'

Mitchell grinned. 'You've got as long as you're getting something useful. I'll go and tell the boss where you are. If he's not pleased, I'll fetch you in time for his meeting. I'll come in with you to carry the blankets.'

The heat enfolded them as they entered and looked round. Notices covered the walls, written in thick black pen on luminous colours. Their quarry sat beneath the least friendly. Sharing a large orange poster, two commands forbade customers to consume their purchases from the fish and chip shop next door on these premises, and not to use the phone number at the bottom for any reason other than a breakdown.

Mrs Staniforth, unaware of either the two officers or any of the notices, was reaching up to her waist into the drum of a giant washing machine, her rear end bustling. Mitchell stood, clutching his rugs and staring in bewilderment at the list of instructions on the dry-cleaning machine. Then he dropped and trod on one rug as he fished in his pocket for the right change.

Mrs Staniforth, her clothes loaded and her machine safely switched on, watched him scornfully. 'I should've thought the police'd be able to afford a washing machine.'

Jennifer explained the task they had in mind, adding, 'Twin babies! Everything's always a mess.'

As she had hoped, Mrs Staniforth melted. 'Twins? My goodness, how old are they?'

'Five weeks.' Jennifer sounded prouder than Virginia.

Mrs Staniforth eyed her up and down. 'You soon got your figure back.'

'They're six weeks now,' Mitchell put in faintly.

With babies as her passport to her witness's interest, Jennifer did not disabuse Mrs Staniforth but hoped she would not ask who was minding them.

'I'll collect you at two, then.'

Mitchell made a hasty departure and Mrs Staniforth watched him head swiftly towards the station. 'Your hubby and I met on this murder.'

Jennifer looked impressed. 'Really?' She listened to a garbled account of Mitchell's visit to her on Saturday afternoon with every appearance of interest and enjoyment, providing an occasional further interpolation of 'Really!' and, once, 'What a responsibility for you.' She hoped they would reach the significant point in the story before both their machines clattered to the end of their programmes. At last, Mrs Staniforth reached the phone call.

'Young people are so thoughtless about using the phone, aren't they? I expect she was on for ages.'

'You're right, she was.'

'She might even have made more than one call.'

'I wouldn't have put it past her, but I don't think she did. She was talking all the time to one person – at least she was when she wasn't giggling. Not that I was listening in.'

'Well, I don't suppose you had much choice but to hear some of it. I mean, you'd have turned the telly down out of politeness so that she could hear whoever she was talking to. I expect it was a boyfriend.'

'Definitely. You could tell from the sort of flighty voice.'

Jennifer nodded with a middle-aged scorn for the young. Had she really said 'telly'? She looked round in alarm at the machine to which she had entrusted Ginny's blankets. It was making disgusting noises and emitting an unhealthy smell.

Mrs Staniforth looked at it too and sniffed. 'They call that progress. Whatever happened to soapsuds?' They embarked on a technical discussion of the merits of water versus cleaning fluids for use on heavy wool until Jennifer pulled herself up. She was enjoying her role so much it was distracting her from the purpose of it. 'I expect, when that girl rang off, you'd lost the thread of the programme you were watching.'

Mrs Staniforth tossed her head. 'I'd only seen three or four minutes of it. I'd been doing the washing-up. No offer of help, of course. She was watching with Fred. Actually, she seemed quite interested.'

'Was it one of those Australian soaps?'

'No, it was just the ITV news. Anyway, out she went to make her call when it was over, and a quarter of an hour later she was off.'

'Do you know which bus she caught?'

Mrs Staniforth snorted over her shoulder as her machine jolted to a halt. She opened the door and began to fold the wet garments rapidly and stack them in her plastic basket. 'Young folk these days don't catch buses. She said she'd get a taxi from the end of the road.'

Jennifer wondered whether to help with folding the bigger items but decided that she would get it wrong and spoil the gossip. Instead she remarked, 'You must have had a dreadful shock when you found out what had happened to the girl.' She was surprised to see Mrs Staniforth begin to transfer the washing to the tumble-dryer. Why had she folded it? Possibly because it would have been lazy not to. The woman paused to say, over her shoulder, 'Not really. Soon as I clapped eyes on her, I said to Fred, "She'll come to a sticky end, that one. Got it written all over her." '

An agonized whine gave way to a final clatter and the dry-cleaning machine was silent. In the timed minute she had to wait before the door could be opened, Jennifer turned over in her mind the burden of Mrs Staniforth's tale, sorting out what might possibly and what simply could not be true. Then, trying not to breathe in the noxious fumes of the cleaning fluid, she shook out Virginia's car rugs. She was thankful that they seemed to have come to no harm. They were no cleaner, chiefly because, apart from Mitchell's foot-print, they had been spotless when they went in.

Chapter Twelve

Mitchell, visiting Dr James Enright in his grand but rather run-down house only half a mile from Kingsgate, wondered how he ever found anything in the confusion of books and papers, piled haphazard on all visible surfaces. He had come to the door promptly, agreed that Mitchell's visit was convenient and led him to a small office off the hall. He provided Mitchell with a seat by sweeping books from a chair to the floor, then went to sit behind his desk.

His sombre outfit, ribbed black shirt with a zip and dark-grey trousers, was enlivened by a crimson wool jacket. Mitchell settled himself comfortably and studied the bony, hollow-cheeked face. The hair, grey-streaked, rather thin and straggly and secured at the back of his head with a rubber band, at least had a shine that came from being recently washed. Thick brows shadowed eyes that were narrowed so that their colour was difficult to discern. Mitchell thought he would be attractive to women.

Needled at being surveyed from behind Enright's desk, Mitchell made him wait for the interview to begin, turning his gaze to a photograph of Ruth that hung over the fireplace. After a moment, he got up and went to stand in front of it. It was clever, managing to capture both the girl's physical fragility and her mental strength. Her dark colouring was softened by the soft peach tone of the garment she wore. It appeared to be a dressing gown, the impression strengthened by the girl's dishevelled hair that was pushed back against the way it would naturally fall. Mitchell could not imagine that she would have turned up to be professionally photographed in such attire.

He turned to Enright, who seemed not at all put out by the silence. 'Did you take this? It's very good and very flattering.'

Enright bridled. 'It's as she is. I think it's very typical.'

Mitchell came to sit down again. 'Hobby of yours, photography?' Enright nodded. 'Do you develop your own?'

He hesitated. 'Well, I started to learn at one time, joined the student society, but I wasn't too handy at it. Anyway, once I've captured what I want with the camera, I lose interest, so that's as far as I go now.'

'It seems a waste of expensive equipment.'

He shook his head. 'I never got round to buying any. I gave up whilst I was still using the students' stuff. How can I help you with your enquiries? Two of the girls were my students, for my sins.'

'What were they like, as students?'

Enright tilted his chair back at a perilous angle. 'Marianne was the type you used to be able to expect. When she came up she was well read, within the limits of someone just out of school, and she read widely in her three years here. She would have taken finals this summer. I was hoping for a first, but realistically expecting an upper second.'

'What was her intended career?'

Enright shrugged. 'I know she was set against teaching. She said it wore you down and she was right. I believe she was considering journalism. Eventually I thought she might have produced some serious novels. She had an original mind and an active imagination and considerable insight into the human mind and personality, considering her youth. A conventional degree course in English doesn't offer much scope for creativity, but it was there. She had the sort of mind I envied.'

'And Paula?'

Enright's lip curled. 'She was an utter moron. I suspect that she slept with her English teacher to get the reference he sent us and with her examiners in order to scrape through her A levels.'

'And what did she sleep with you for?' When he blustered angrily, Mitchell went on serenely. 'All right. Instead, you can tell us what your car was doing outside number seven Kingsgate on Saturday afternoon. When I spoke to you on Sunday you omitted to mention this visit. One of Marianne's customers, were you, come for a quickie whilst Ruth was safely out of the way?'

Enright sighed. 'Ruth's told me what she told you on Sunday. She doesn't know I was anything to do with it. I went along there to try to make sure that it stayed that way.' He came from behind the desk and perched on the corner of it to look into Mitchell's face. 'Look, since I most certainly never harmed those girls, I want to cooperate with you fully, but I can't have Ruth finding out.'

Mitchell edged his chair away before giving a qualified assurance. 'I shan't tell her, but no one can say what might eventually come out in court. You'd do better to tell her yourself.'

'It stopped as soon as I met her. I was rather smitten with Marianne when she first came up but all she wanted from me was enrolment on her books. That was how I met Ruth. I was taking Paula back to her digs. Marianne frowned on that, but Paula was drunk.'

'What exactly were you doing there on Saturday?'

'Ruth—'

'Was in Nottingham.'

'I just wanted to—'

'Cooperate fully, I think you said.'

'I wanted to see Paula, talk some sense into her. She was threatening to tell Ruth about us if I didn't make sure she got enough marks in the half-sessionals to be able to continue her course. But I didn't harm her. She wasn't there. None of them was.'

Browne faced Babasola Ogunade across the interview room table and recognized what Winters had described as 'that clever-clever expression' on the handsome black face. 'You're not going to miss the chance to pin this on a nigger.'

Browne smiled. 'I've heard that's a word you're fond of. We're not allowed to use it, I'm afraid. We actually prefer it when our criminals turn out not to be black. It avoids the complication of having them, their friends and the press screaming prejudice however much proof of their guilt we might have.'

'But since I've done no harm to any of those girls, you can't have any against me.'

Ogunade, at his request, had been provided with a change of his clothes. 'Even he,' Winters had observed, 'draws the line at being interviewed wearing the loot.' He now wore khaki shorts and a yellow T-shirt under a loose, multicoloured cotton top of pseudo-African design. His choice of clothing probably made him more comfortable in this windowless, overheated interview room than Caroline and himself in their winter outfits. Jesus sandals completed the native effect. Browne half wondered if his suspect would speak in pidgin English to add verisimilitude but Ogunade used his usual voice, the almost pure BBC with its faint hint of the West Midlands. 'Harborne, perhaps,' had been the suggestion of the PC who stood by the door and who had been raised in Aston.

'Your teachers describe you as an intelligent student. I wouldn't have expected you to persist in denying—'

'I've already owned to taking the stuff from the houses in Crossley Bridge. The ram-raid that produced all the electrical goods was entirely the brainchild of Dez and Cracker, carried out against my advice.'

'You're talking about Desmond Mallet and Callum Crossley?'

'I suppose so. Desmond and Callum?' His tone was wondering. 'I'm not surprised they'll only answer to nicknames . . .'

'Which leaves us with four handbags.'

'About which none of us knows anything.'

'But which were taken from the murder scene on Saturday afternoon and found on Sunday, in a shed to which only you have a key.'

'If you say so.'

'I do, and I'd like an explanation.'

'And so would I. If you'll share it with me when you've found it, I'll be greatly obliged to you.'

Browne seldom lost his temper these days and never when he was being deliberately provoked. 'Tell me something about yourself.' His tone was that of the chairman of an interviewing committee to his preferred candidate.

Ogunade's smile flashed whitely. 'Certainly. What would you like to know? I'm a second-year chemist at Bradford, born in Birmingham. My father came from Nigeria in 1970. My mother was born in Bradford. I'm an only son with two sisters.' He paused politely to check if this information was what was wanted.

Browne's face was rapt. 'Hobbies?'

'Quite a lot. Running, soccer, photography, playing drums, bit of burglary now and then. That finances the rest and you have to have some excitement.'

'Girlfriend?'

'I haven't let a particular one pin me down, but I'm normal and girls seem not to dislike my company.'

'Including the girls who were murdered?'

'I'd socialized with them all except the much older one.'

'Rather more than socialized, unless the word has a technical sense that I'm not familiar with.' Browne nodded to the constable who opened the door to admit DC Craig.

Craig placed the handbags he was carrying on the table and addressed Ogunade. 'Open that one.' He indicated a bulging imitation-crocodile pouch with a peeling gilt metal fastener. His manner slightly less assured, Ogunade reached towards it, clicked it open and watched as it disgorged a small cascade of cosmetics. 'If you undo the zipped compartment, you'll find a letter, addressed to yourself. It has a first-class stamp on it, which is rather a waste now it's being hand-delivered. Of course, as a gentleman, I hate reading other people's correspondence. Since we had to read yours in the course of our duty I thought the least I could do was bring it to you and let you read it too.'

Suddenly, Browne was tired of Craig's schoolboy humour. 'Just open the letter, Mr Ogunade.' The man obeyed, his face impassive. 'Would you like to tell us what it says, for the sake of the tape recorder?'

Ogunade read to the end of the two sheets, then looked up. 'It's a page and a half of inarticulate hysteria but it boils down to an accusation that I was responsible for her pregnancy.'

'And were you?'

'Along with about a dozen others I could have been.'

'So you had good reason to want one of the four girls out of the way.'

Ogunade was unmoved. 'Possibly, if I'd known about it, but the burglaries which I'm not denying were quite lucrative. I could have afforded to contribute one twelfth of the cost of an abortion and I would have positively enjoyed making sure that the other eleven paid their share.'

Edward's photographs were now completely dry and he had gathered them into a pile. It didn't matter that there were only thirty-six. He was a much better photographer now than last time. The last exposure, the view from the sitting-room doorway, had turned out to be his favourite as he had known it would.

He held it up to the light from the attic window. At a first glance it showed just a social gathering, but, when you looked again, there was a lack of animation about the figures – naturally. He giggled at his play on words, then took himself firmly in hand.

No one, of course, was actually drinking, holding a cup. They were sitting like dolls that some little girl had placed on chairs to have a pretend tea party, except, of course, that there was delicate china, not a plastic toy teaset, gleaming white with contrasting dark-red flowers and green leaves and lavish gold-leaf edging. Alive, they had only been dolls, except for Jo, perhaps; mindless and spiteful dolls. And now they had had their punishment and he had the record of it to satisfy his sense of justice.

They had not been sorry for laughing at him, for being a threat to his reputation, but he had not let them spoil all his plans. He began pinning up his new pictures underneath the old ones. There had only been three girls that other time, not so clearly delineated, nor so artistically arranged, but they were a good enough representation to make him feel again the surge of satisfaction he had felt at the time he had brought them to justice, made them pay for the times they had made him pay. He smiled grimly, then turned to the opposite wall.

Here, well away from the rest so that they would not contaminate, were pictures of his truly loved, his unattainable woman. Rows and rows of them. An occasional one taken, like this one, with her knowledge. He stood before it, then reached out to touch it, pull it from its little blob of Blu-Tack and hold it in his hand. He let his eyes linger in turn on each feature of the figure in the picture, the tumble of thick, dark-brown wavy hair, the ice-cool blue of eyes not quite smiling, contrasting with the sun-burnished golden skin.

He had enlarged this one to emphasize how the clinging ribbed sweater outlined the swell of the breasts and narrowed itself at the slim waist, the whole shape tantalizingly half hidden behind the huge collar and lapels of the jacket. The long, slender legs were chastely encased in shiny leggings, the small feet in neat ankle boots.

Edward's hand trembled as he replaced the picture. It was his favourite because she had granted it. Many of the other pictures were more revealing but less pleasing because he had cheated, taken them without permission, exulting in what the telephoto lens revealed to him to take away and enjoy, but silently craving her pardon for the liberty he had taken. He looked at a row of these secret studies, bare legs and shoulders, brief scraps of satin and lace. They excited him but none of them roused him almost to worship her as the one he had enlarged always did.

She never called him Edward, nor Jack either, as the first collection of girls had. Jack had been his father's name. Useful enough as an alias but he preferred Edward, his more studied choice. It meant 'rich guardian'. An old and royal name. Sometimes he'd thought of giving *her* a name too, one that only he would use, but he didn't feel he could presume to choose for *her*. He couldn't be sure that the names he considered hadn't been contaminated, been taken by the sort of female he was obliged to use and then had to punish for her part in his degradation.

This time he had no handbags to add to his collection. He felt upset at the moment that the police had appropriated this property of his, and that he was in no position to claim it back. He had realized since he had lost them, though, that it was many months since he had opened those other girls' bags, sorted through and handled the contents. In time, he thought the loss would seem unimportant. He had had to take them from the scene on Saturday, of course, his trophies, to prove his authority over Briony, Paula and Marianne. Jo's bag he hadn't really needed. The only manner in which she had offended him was by being, inconveniently, there.

He finished pinning up the rest of the new pictures before turning for a last look at *her.* As he feasted his eyes, a female voice rose from the floor below. 'Your tea is ready. Whatever are you doing up there?' He walked down the stairs very slowly, letting the effect the excitement had had on his body die away before it could betray him.

When Mitchell had collected Jennifer from Washing World, it had been with a message to go straight to Barry Parker's house to interview his daughter. She was delighted to find that Stephanie was at home alone. Her stepmother, she said, was meeting the boys from school and taking them into town to buy new shoes. Her father was 'out', uncompromisingly without explanation.

Jennifer took the Coke and the kitchen stool she was offered. 'That's fine. It was you I wanted to talk to.'

Stephanie stared at the floor. 'Yes, I know. Are you going to take me to court?'

Jennifer blinked, then rallied. 'That depends on quite a lot of things. Suppose you give me your version of what happened? I'll have a better idea of what line we think it's right to take when we've got an all-round picture.' As the girl worked out how to explain her situation, putting herself in the best light, Jennifer covertly examined her.

A spiral perm and a bottle of bleach had combined to give a first impression that she was not at all like her elder brother, but a second glance showed a face very like the one in the photograph Mitchell had passed round, fine-boned with a defenceless expression and the same way of ducking the head so that the eyes were shadowed. She was rather elaborately made up for an afternoon at home. The clothes were casual but the trousers were well cut and must have been expensive.

After a silence of some seconds, Jennifer decided to make a stab in the dark. The girl was at home at three o'clock in the afternoon. 'You're unemployed, of course.'

'Well, what do you think? I am now. No second chances from Mr Cooper.'

'What exactly did your job involve?'

Stephanie had relaxed a little now that the conversation was under way. She attacked the ring-pull of her can and took a swig of the fizzy contents. 'Just the usual stuff they let students do, shelf-filling, tidying up.'

'Quite hard work, I imagine. Tins of beans are heavy.'

The girl fiddled with the ring-pull which she had dropped on to the table. 'I'm not bothered about losing the job. What they paid wouldn't have gone far to pay off my debts but at least it showed I was doing my best.'

'And how much do you owe altogether? Are you sure you've told us everything?'

'As much as I can remember. I've lost count.' Diluted mascara trickled down her cheeks. At least, Jennifer noted, her make-up was not top-of-the-range.

'Right. Now, describe exactly how you fell foul of Mr Cooper.'

Stephanie banged her can down angrily. 'Not by ripping him off like some of the others do! It was my first day there. I took a few cartons of tins and things home, stuff Debbie wanted. I kept her money.'

'Debbie?'

'My stepmother. She doesn't know anything about it all. I'm eighteen so I don't have to tell my parents – at least, not yet.'

'Stephanie.' Jennifer waited until the girl looked up at her. 'Actually, I was sent to see you because there's something else you can help us with.'

She cheered up immediately. 'Will it get me off the hook if I do?'

Jennifer shook her head. 'It's not in my power to decide, but it can't do you any harm.'

'But you will tell them I've been cooperative?'

'If I think you have been.'

The information poured out. No, she had not heard from Jon since he ran off but she was quite sure that Cracker would know where he was. No, she was not afraid of her brother. He was a bit of a wimp, actually. He'd left this house after a fight they'd had five years ago.

Jennifer interrupted her. 'Fight? I thought he'd made an attack on you.'

She laughed mirthlessly. 'That's how Dad told it. He wanted Jon out.'

'Why?'

'Because he didn't like it that Dad was sleeping with me.'

As Jennifer parked the Fiesta outside her house a couple of hours later, the former differences between herself and Paul had been cut down to size. She felt only thankfulness for the sweet wholesomeness of the life they had had together. She would have taken back not one jot of her defence of her rights, but she tempered her indignation now with appreciation. Paul had been an attentive and patient father who had delighted in the prospect of their second child and loved dearly the one he already had, for all she showed promise of making her mother's rebellion look like willing subjection.

Lucy danced down the hall to meet her now, clean and shining from her bath, her curtain of dark hair reaching to the belt of her dressing gown. Jennifer kissed her and grinned over the child's head at her mother-in-law who stood in the living-room doorway, a finger to her lips. 'I wish I could believe she's been as angelic as she looks.'

Lucy pulled away from her mother and considered solemnly. 'I was a bit naughty but I said sorry and Granny Jane said it was all right.'

Jennifer looked sharply back to find Granny Jane winking at her daughter. 'You heard. Apology accepted. All forgiven and forgotten. I promised they could both stay up to see you but Judith didn't make it. She's asleep in the chair, but at least you can carry her up and tuck her in.'

Coming downstairs again, Jennifer realized from the smells escaping from the kitchen that supper was to be Mexican, Jane's speciality. Lucy watched hopefully as her mother ate. 'I like hot spicy food.'

'She does too.' The child flashed her grandmother a warning look and saw that she was not to be betrayed.

Jennifer emptied her loaded fork into her daughter's mouth. 'That's your lot. I've been working hard and I'm hungry.'

Lucy knew when she was wasting her time and retired to her half-completed jigsaw on the floor. The two women chatted as Jennifer finished her meal.

'Yes, I usually watch the local news.'

'You don't happen to remember what was on last Friday?'

Jane shook her head. 'The programmes merge together in your mind after a bit. There was something on about a choir from Doncaster at the end of last week. That might have been Friday. They'd won some competition. Why do you want to know?'

Jennifer explained and they passed to other matters, then fell into silence.

'Penny for them?' Jane demanded as Jennifer laid down her knife and fork.

'I was almost falling asleep.' Jennifer apologized

hastily. She could hardly explain to Paul's mother, in the hearing of his daughter, that she had been giving thanks for her certainty that there were no circumstances in which Paul would ever have taken advantage of his daughters in any way.

Suspecting that the highlight of his wife's day had been bundling offspring numbers 2, 3 and 4 into the car to go and collect number 1, Mitchell did his utmost to keep awake and entertain her with an account of his day.

Virginia listened with interest, occasionally putting in a comment or question. 'What were you hoping the vicar would tell you about the organist?'

'I was hoping he'd be given a watertight alibi, though I didn't expect it. Cavill Jackson was alone at Kingsgate for some time, by his own admission. Then I hoped the reverend would say that such a crime was completely against his character, but I didn't get that assurance either.'

'You like him. What about the lecturer then?'

Mitchell shook his head. 'I really can't see him as our man, unless he got furious because they were all trying to put his young girlfriend off marrying him.'

'But if he killed everyone who warned her off marrying someone twenty years older, he'd have to do away with half the population of Cloughton.'

'Well, four at one go would be a good start. Come to think of it, it's the only motive that's been suggested so far that applies to all four girls. What's for supper?'

Virginia's manner became defensive. 'They've led me a dance today – the twins, I mean. The other two know better. I haven't planned anything. You wouldn't like to fetch a takeaway, would you?' Relieved, Mitchell expressed sympathy for her predicament and enthusiasm for curry.

Later, fortified by lamb korma, his father-in-law's home-brew and his own excellent coffee, he asked her, 'Do you remember the other day when we were talking about my inspector's exams?'

'Yes. You've been doing your studying, haven't you? I've kept the kids out of your way whenever you went upstairs.'

'It isn't that. You said you agreed with everything I'd said except one.' She nodded. 'So, what was the exception?'

'You said you'd become a sergeant by default.'

'Well, I did.'

'No you didn't. I heard the Super saying to Dad that they'd been damned lucky to appoint you.'

'That's right, lucky someone who knew what was going on locally could step in quickly when Jerry was taken ill again.'

'Idiot! You must know it doesn't work like that. There must have been dozens of applications for Jerry's job. The fact that you weren't fresh blood went against you. The fact that your DCI is my father went against you even more. In spite of all that the powers that be appointed you and turned down all the others. I'm going to make some tea. Shall I bring in another bottle?'

Mitchell stoutly turned his back on temptation. 'No, I'd better keep a clear head. When I came in I thought I was too tired to study, but I must have been hungry. If you don't mind being left with your book, I think I'll put in an hour.'

Virginia retired, her object achieved. Benny was back on course for his next promotion.

Chapter Thirteen

As he waited on Tuesday morning for his team to report, Browne wondered how to inject a little fresh enthusiasm into the investigation. He dared not drop the house-to-house enquiries, but the first useful flow of information had dried up and it was less likely now that any vital facts would emerge. His men had produced a wealth of theories about the murders, likely and unlikely, but there was nothing yet to support any particular one rather than the others, and they were in the mood now to abandon all of them. Even the keenest officer felt disinclined to study the statements they had already been given when the man they sought was just as likely to be someone they had not yet even heard of. He could be any one of the myriad employed by the university. He wondered if they had been right in their assumption that Jo Merry was the one of the four who had lost her life just because she had happened to be at home when the killer collected up the others. Their killer might possibly be someone she had met through her television programme whose primary aim had been to get rid of her. It was not very likely, though. He was becoming as fanciful as his son-in-law.

As though summoned by Browne's musings, Mitchell knocked and entered, the first as usual but quickly followed by the rest. Too quickly, before he had had time to give him a full report on his latest grandchildren.

Browne opened the proceedings himself, reporting on his further questioning of Ogunade and the information he had been given by Blain and Paters, Jo Merry's solicitors. With the exception of small legacies to Ruth Roberts and a certain Michael Vincent who would have to be found and questioned, her whole estate had been left to Cavill Jackson. There was a short silence as the men considered the implications of this not totally unexpected news, broken, of course, by Mitchell.

'Do we have the other PM reports?'

Browne nodded. 'There are copies in the file. None of the other girls was pregnant. Jo Merry, in fact, was a virgin.' A murmur went round the gathering. 'Same cause of death in each case, Paula's around midmorning on Saturday and Marianne's in the early afternoon. Someone from the lab has made us a sketch of the chain marks that you'd all better see.'

Browne invited Mitchell to report on his conversations with Tony Kirkbride and James Enright. '. . . Enright says he only slept with one of the victims, Paula, though he'd used various other girls on the list. I wish we could find Marianne's list of customers. Have we enough to search Enright's place? That's possibly what he went to Kingsgate for on Saturday.'

Browne shook his head. 'I don't think so yet. Anyway, it'll have been destroyed – if it ever existed!'

'It might,' Jennifer put in, 'have been locked into Jo Merry's computer, if Marianne was daring enough.'

'And if she knew enough about computers.' Browne was sceptical. 'She couldn't just leave it on a list of available files. Did you try Enright for the names of other customers?'

'He says he doesn't know and that the name Edward means nothing to him. That's someone Ruth Roberts mentioned,' he added to a puzzled-looking Craig.

Given her turn to report, Jennifer diffidently produced her four columns of facts and questions before passing on what she had learned about Stephanie Parker's serious debts to her bank, her college and a hire-purchase company. She described the girl's abuse by her father from the age of twelve.

'How on earth did he get custody?' Winters demanded.

'Because she never talked about it. She doesn't seem to object to the arrangement. Apparently the abuse stopped some time last year. If she feels anything about that, it seems to be offence at his neglect.'

'So you can't persuade her to press charges?'

Jennifer shook her head. 'She's had an abortion that her father arranged last year, though by then she was more general in her favours and she couldn't be sure that the child was his. That's probably why the father left her alone.'

'So why is she so forthcoming now?'

Jennifer looked sheepish. 'Because she thought I'd come about the stealing she's been doing from the local supermarket, and she thinks if she cooperates with us she won't be prosecuted. Apparently Jonathan was thrown out because he tackled his father on Stephanie's behalf. He did it privately because both he and Stephanie are very fond of their little brothers and grateful to their stepmother. She seems to care about them considerably more than their real mother.'

'Just a minute!' All eyes turned to Craig. 'Where does Jonathan's attack on his sister fit in?'

'When he got nowhere remonstrating with his father, he pleaded with Stephanie. She wouldn't listen. He called her a few foul names, asked if she was available for the whole family. She laughed and said there was nothing to fear from him because he hadn't got the bottle. He lost his temper and slapped her around a bit. When she was examined, it was obvious that she'd been roughly sexually assaulted over a long period. Jon took the rap to save his stepmother's feelings. He thinks she and Cavill Jackson are the only people who care whether he lives or dies.'

There was a long silence before Craig said, with disappointment, 'So there's no link between young Parker and the murders?'

Jennifer was not so sure. 'He must be a pretty disturbed boy. Stephanie seems to know Ogunade. She was going to tell me about him when her stepmother arrived back with the boys. I'm seeing her again today.'

Browne had been silent for some time. Now he

asked, 'Does her family know about the bother at the supermarket?'

'Apparently not. She's hoping they won't and that I'm her ticket to all that fizzling out.' Jennifer looked at her DCI hopefully but he was listening to Mitchell's request for a check to be made on the movements of Ruth Roberts on Saturday. She kept quiet. After all, she had much enjoyed her almond tart.

Rory Jackson lived on an estate of council houses that had mostly been sold to their tenants. Jackson's seemed to have been given that hurried but well-meaning attention that is what can be spared by responsible but very busy people. The paint was peeling in places but was well washed. The lawn had been cut and the borders weeded before the dead of winter had begun, but hedge-clipping had been missed and the garden was surrounded by shaggy, branching privet.

Jackson let Mitchell into the living room, where he was keeping an eye on his youngest offspring, not yet old enough for school. He was an older, tired-looking, less colourful version of Cavill. There were no red tints in his brown hair, the eyes were a lighter blue and his face paler and sallower. According to Kirkbride, this brother was the elder by nine years, Mitchell reflected. Probably his work, though just as satisfying, was more demanding and less likely to bring either public acclaim or great financial reward.

He seemed relieved rather than disappointed that

Mitchell brought him no news of Jonathan Parker. 'I'm really surprised he's gone off like this. He was enjoying Highfield House and they thought he was doing well. If you pick him up on a job, there'll be absolutely nothing I can do. It would be another stretch, no questions asked and I don't think anyone could reclaim him after that.'

'Is he worth all this concern?'

Jackson shrugged and prevented his small son from crashing a model truck into the table leg. 'My job is to support my clients, not pass judgement on them, but yes, I think he is, considering everything.'

'What's everything?'

Jackson wandered over to the window and glared out of it at the untidy sprouting hedge. He spoke without turning back. 'When I look back on my own teenage years, I remember support and tolerance of my misdemeanours. Up to about the age of twenty-one I lived in a protected time zone, at school and university. I had middle-class friends who carried Swiss Army knives for fun, not self-defence, and I couldn't swear that none of them ever tried drugs.'

'Is Jon on drugs?'

'He says not. I've no proof either way. I don't know whether I believe him or not. What I do know is how little support he has from his family. His chief ties are to his friends. These lads hit the streets and behave as young males have done down the ages. They establish their own territory, fight when they're insulted or threatened. They have no army training or university sports clubs to absorb their aggression. We expect them to respect a system of justice that has condemned them . . .'

Mitchell knew that Jackson would have to finish this recital of his social creed before he could be brought back to matters more relevant to his own investigation. He winked at the little boy as his father's rolling phrases echoed round them both. 'Tycoons . . . millions . . . university students . . . drinking and lying in bed . . . twelve thousand a year for Eton, twenty thousand to keep a man in prison . . . just eight thousand subsidy for each boy on this course . . . persistent offenders . . . last chance . . . rigorously structured ten-week programme.'

Now the hedge outside was beginning to irritate Mitchell too. One of six children, brought up in a five-roomed house, his mother's rule had been that a job was done the minute it needed doing. One of the few subjects of contention between Ginny and himself was her somewhat casual attitude to household tasks. He turned back to Jackson, who had reached the philosophy behind the training at Highfield House. 'They maintain that crimes are choices . . . examine the boys' innate sense of right and wrong . . . pick the crime of which each of them is most ashamed and draw it out as a cartoon, frame by frame.'

'I'll bring my hedge cutter round if you like. Plug it in and it'd tidy that lot up in no time.'

'What? Oh, that's good of you. Thanks. Sorry, I'm keen on this work but I know I tend to go on about it a bit.'

'No. Go on.' The tape recorder in Mitchell's head

had just played back to him Jackson's last few phrases. 'Are you telling me that Jon's tutors gave him an exercise to do that involved drawing a strip cartoon of one of their offences?'

'That's right. They have to pick out at exactly which point they could have made another choice.'

Mitchell held up his hand, grinning. 'For Pete's sake, don't start again. Just listen for a minute.' He explained briefly the misunderstanding that had led Beryl Parker to lose her temper and drive her volatile son back, so far as anyone knew, to his former companions and their life of petty crime. Jackson grew excited, certain that the staff of Highfield House would understand the boy's indignation at his mother's lack of trust. 'If we can find him quickly I'm almost sure I can get them to take him back.'

Mitchell supplied the addresses of Dez and Cracker as possible starting points for Jackson's search. 'Well, now you've told me what I wanted to know and I've given you what help I can, but my boss actually sent me here to ask you about your brother.'

'Cavill? Well, Highfield House runs classes in various arts and crafts to back up all the work I've been telling you about. Jon's all fingers and thumbs with a paintbrush and he's a bit timid in contact sports, although he's a nifty runner, so I persuaded Cavill to start him off on the organ. Once he'd met him Cavill took no more persuading. They got on well both socially and . . .' Jackson's voice tailed off as it became obvious to him that this was not what Mitchell wanted.

'I'm supposed to get you to give me the sort of

rundown on your brother that you've just given me on Parker, especially any connection he had with Jo Merry and her student guests.'

'You can piss off!'

Mitchell was unruffled. 'That's precisely what I'd say if someone was being nosy about my brother too. But you still have to answer my question.'

Stephanie Parker presented herself to Jennifer five minutes before she was due. She wore an armour of make-up and a Jacques Vert suit and proved just as ready as she had been the day before to tell everything that the police might want to know.

She thought it unlikely that Jonathan knew any of the murdered girls. 'But I did. Briony was in my business studies class and we used to see each other evenings as well, quite a bit.'

'You mentioned Sola Ogunade yesterday. How well do you know him?'

'It depends what you mean by knowing. I met him a couple of months ago at a uni disco. Our college isn't part of the university but you can get into the union building if you know the right people. I've seen him once or twice since, always with a different girl. Then, last Wednesday, Bri and I went to another disco and Sola and Bri had a big row. He ended up with me that night but nothing happened.'

'You mean you didn't sleep with him?'

'No. I don't know what went wrong.' Jennifer cast her eyes up to the ceiling, wondering at the ethical code that had to seek a reason why a girl failed to end up in bed with a scarcely known dancing partner. She shut out the salutary thought that shaking her head at the morals of the young was a sure sign of the passing of her own youth.

Stephanie was shaking her head. 'But I did on Saturday. We arranged to meet on Sunday but he didn't turn up.'

'No, I'm afraid we were entertaining him.'

Stephanie greeted this news with a smile of satisfaction. Jennifer removed it with her next question. 'What about Briony?'

'I'm not sure. I think he'd finished with her. When I told him on Saturday that she was going to name him as her baby's father he said she couldn't, he'd shut her mouth for her.'

'You mean he *would* shut it, or he *had*?'

She shrugged. 'I can't remember.'

'What do you think he meant by it?'

'*I* don't know. That he'd drop her in it, I suppose, if she said anything.'

'Drop her in it?'

Stephanie obviously pitied Jennifer's slow wits. 'Tell her other bloke she was pregnant.'

'Wouldn't he find out anyway before long?'

Stephanie was amused. 'You don't think she was going to *have* it? She wanted getting-rid money plus a bit extra for the inconvenience and for not making a complaint to his college.'

'And was Sola going to pay up?'

'He didn't say. It wouldn't have been the end of the world for Briony. She wasn't hard up.'

'Rich parents?'

Stephanie shook her head. 'No way. Anyway, she wouldn't go to them for abortion money.'

'She had a job then?'

'You could say so.'

'Bar work?'

Stephanie gave a mirthless laugh. 'That's where it often started off, I suppose.'

Jennifer's tone became less friendly. 'We know all about how Briony and the other girls earned their money.'

Stephanie too changed her expression. 'Well, perhaps you can tell me what Marianne had against employing *me*.'

Cavill Jackson watched through the leaded window of the choir vestry as the boys began to arrive for practice. The metamorphosis from street urchin to exemplary chorister occurred about halfway across the car park, in front of the church hall and alongside the vestry door. Wheelies stopped and the young cyclists took their machines carefully to the corner where they quietly padlocked them to a convenient rail. Those on foot tumbled and screamed through the gate but walked decorously past the hall to the vestry.

They went there only to pick up hymn books. Cavill never insisted on cassocks for practice. The local youth club opened its doors three streets away before the singing finished. The boys stayed willingly before careering off for the second half of the table-tennis and disco session and he was not going to push his luck by keeping them back for disrobing.

He felt rather like a headless chicken as he went into church, his mind far away but his body automatically going through all the motions of his normal life. It occurred to him that perhaps by most people's standards his life was not very normal, but he was getting back to managing to do what was normal for him, planning the programmes of services and performances, coaxing, encouraging and, occasionally, berating the boys.

Tonight, nothing had been consciously planned. As he stood in front of the choir they drew from him what they expected and needed. He remembered a conversation he had had with his sister-in-law on the subject of raising his nephew and nieces. 'I don't consciously give them any kind of treatment,' she had told him, when he had asked if she treated them all alike. 'They take what they need. It's enough that I don't resent it. That's what love is.'

She must have meant parental love. It wasn't the kind of love he had had for Jo – if he had loved her at all. She wouldn't take what she needed. She had been rebuffed too often and had resorted to persuading herself that she needed nothing so as to avoid any more humiliation. He supposed he had been trying to make her vulnerable again, trying to convince her that if she risked herself, she would eventually find a relationship that would compensate her for all the wounding.

But when she had begun to look for that response from him he had resented it. Latterly, he had resented it a great deal. He blinked, forced his mind to return to the immediate present and decided that the following Sunday's Matins with Communion, and its hymns, canticles and anthem had been sufficiently rehearsed in just half an hour.

Cavill had been surprised and dismayed by the absence of five boys tonight. The media would have supplied all the choir parents with the news of the four girls' murder in Kingsbury, and the parish grapevine would have informed them of his own connection with one of them and the police interest in him. Had they tried and condemned him?

He wondered whether to ask about the absentees but decided against this. He seldom encouraged the boys to tell tales of one another and tried not to take advantage of the delightful indiscretion of his probationers in particular. Their parents, he knew, would be astonished and painfully embarrassed if they realized half what he knew about them through the candid comments of their sons.

He was especially vigilant in his dealings with the Parker boys. Benjie was too young really to be here at all, and his parents had not done anything to help prepare him. Nevertheless the boy's innate musical ability was pushing him to cope with the problems of self-control and the reading of both words and notes that were keeping him from full membership.

If he had had Jon Parker at this age he was sure he could have saved him. In fact, he felt certain that their contact with the church choir was keeping at least three of his boys from nefarious activities which might soon have them in police hands. It was giving them something to value in themselves.

He gave out his own choir notices, praise for the way they had coped with the last-minute substitutions of anthem and hymns last Sunday and news of the invitation he had received for them to take part in a weekend festival for boys' choirs to be held in Wakefield Cathedral later in the year. The invitation delighted them as it had himself. 'You're the only non-cathedral choir to be asked,' he told them. 'That should make you all very proud of yourselves. We're all to sing Evensong together each night, and on the Saturday there will be a concert. Each of the four choirs will have twenty minutes of it to fill. That should give scope for at least one piece that everyone likes. You can make suggestions, written please, and you must put your name on the paper.' He looked hard at Reuben. 'Otherwise, I might get ten from one person and use them all, and then no one else would have had a say.'

The boys were obviously anticipating the occasion with unalloyed pleasure. They had sung as a visiting choir before but only as day visitors. This time they would be sharing accommodation with upper-middle-class cathedral-choir schoolboys. Oh well, they'd have each other, and education had to be painful sometimes.

He held up a hand to still the chattering. 'Right.

It's listening time.' To a man, they closed their eyes, most of them resting chins in hands, their elbows on the music shelf in front of them. Cavill slipped a CD into his small portable player. This part of the ninety-minute session was his favourite. He was very conscious of the great privilege it was to be responsible for the musical education of these lads, whose experience of it had extended so far only to what was churned out on Radio 1.

Today he was exposing them to the seven and a half minutes of Judith Weir's *Ascending into Heaven*. They received it in a silence which went on for several seconds after the last note died away. Then the irrepressible Kevin Stebbings volunteered, 'It's weird!' Cavill glanced at the lad. Yes, it had been intended as a pun. Wonderful. They were to have a choir wit.

'It's not what you're used to,' he agreed. 'This was written quite recently, only just before you were born.' He realized as he spoke that, to Kevin, a song was out of date if it had been released on record last month.

As the boys listened, several members of the adult choir had been coming in and seating themselves silently. They too had given their attention to the arresting little piece and heard the simple explanation he gave of its salient characteristics. As he removed the disc from the machine, a voice asked, 'Could *we* sing that – for the festival?'

Cavill regarded Paul Parker thoughtfully, considering his suggestion. 'We'll learn it,' he decided, 'but I'm not promising that we'll sing it at the festival until I see how we get on with it.' He was tempted. The boys would love the glissando bars and he himself would enjoy the virtuoso organ accompaniment. He grinned as a tenor from behind remarked, 'It wouldn't be the daftest bloody thing you'd talked us into!'

Cavill looked behind him to invite the tenors and basses and two lady altos to take their places behind the boys. Soon the latter would be released, after just a quick run through the Stanford service they had been practising for some time. The hard work done already, it would be a romp.

He climbed into the organ loft and the music took over as he had known it would, lifted him, demanded from him, bullied him, then glorified him. Cavill hated melodramatic expressions but he could think of no other way to describe what was happening to him. Jo had called it intoxication when she had seen him in this state, but although this captured his abandonment, it gave no idea of his exaltation. When the Te Deum finished, he – and the choir with him – floated back to earth, knowing that they had been somewhere else. They went on to the Jubilate but he felt that here was not the same sureness of touch. He didn't find the same freshness, the same exciting alternation of exuberance and serenity. They enjoyed the sound they were making, but they remained aware that they were standing in the chancel practising a canticle. Still, he felt glad that he had ignored Tony's urgings to cancel his practice for once. He would only have sat at home feeling guilty, and he would have missed all that the singers had given him. Among them tonight, for the second time since walking into that chamber of horrors, he felt real, made of flesh and blood, even hungry and thirsty.

Coming through to the body of the church again, he became aware of a stocky figure standing in the gloom of the Lady chapel. It was not another volunteer tenor. Even before the figure had stepped forward into the light, he had recognized Detective Sergeant Mitchell.

Chapter Fourteen

Cavill Jackson was puzzled as he eyed Mitchell. 'How long have you been there?'

'Long enough.' Mitchell came out into the chancel and the boys whispered excitedly. 'You're doing a good job.'

Jackson seemed pleased. 'Yes, I am, aren't I?' He dismissed the nine juniors and they trooped out of church, turning, as they reached the outside world, into the small tearaways who would harry the youth-club leaders for the rest of the evening.

'How do you get them to come?' Mitchell demanded.

Jackson smiled. 'When I first arrived at St Barnabas' and wanted to form a boys' choir I appealed to the parents. Five boys were brought along to be auditioned, some more willingly than others. At a pinch, they would all have made the grade but I turned three of them down. I made it a majority so they didn't feel humiliated. As soon as little boys are refused something, they want it. The two chosen ones were envied.

'I made them work hard, then I let them sing solo verses in some of the hymns at a service. The next time I held auditions there was a queue right down the aisle. We couldn't do anything very challenging until I'd taught them all to sight-read, but now—'

Mitchell forestalled a long recital of the boys' technical abilities. 'Yes, I heard them.'

Jackson shut and locked the vestry door and leaned back against it. 'After a week or two, one of the new choristers' fathers came to see me. He said he wasn't having his boy turned into a poof. His son, incidentally, is a fine little musician.'

'What happened?'

Jackson's grin broadened. 'The father stayed to hear what went on at practice. Two weeks later he had joined the adult choir as a very useful tenor. I'd told him I could see where the lad's talent came from. By the way, those two youngsters in Leeds United strips are Jon Parker's half-brothers.'

Mitchell glanced through the window but all the boys were now lost to view in the darkness. Jackson dropped on to a vestry chair. 'I once overheard another chorister's father saying, "He runs it like the ruddy army." Actually, I run it loosely on cathedral choir lines, but the army was the only place this father had experienced a similar degree of discipline and had the same kind of commitment demanded of him. I took the remark as a compliment.'

He stopped, reading Mitchell's face. 'You didn't come here for all this, did you? I'd better give the adult choir a night off. None of them has come far.'

'Please.' Whilst he waited for this to be done, Mitchell settled himself more comfortably. Jackson would feel relaxed here, on home ground. 'I came to bring you some news, Mr Jackson – or maybe you know about it already.'

'We won't know till you tell me.'

'Right. Miss Merry's will leaves number seven Kingsgate to you, unmortgaged, plus a sum in excess of three hundred thousand pounds.'

'What?' Jackson stopped pacing round the vestry and stared. 'You mean all that orphanage stuff was lies?' He sank on to the chair next to Mitchell's and shook his head in bewilderment as he listened to an explanation of Jo Merry's situation.

'You're about to become a fairly rich man.'

Jackson looked unimpressed. 'I'm a fairly rich man already. I earn more than I need by my own hands, literally. Whatever would I do with all that? Besides, it lands me in the soup, doesn't it?'

'It does?'

'Well, up to now, all you've had against me was that Jo was my friend and that, for a lot of the time you're interested in, I was either alone at home or alone at church.'

'And, at the vital time, alone at the murder scene.'

'Well, someone had to find them.' Mitchell could not refute this. Jackson was still shaking his head distractedly. 'Will I be able to go to Cologne in a couple of weeks' time?' he asked suddenly. 'I'm booked to do a recital in the cathedral on February the fifth.'

'I shouldn't think so, if the case isn't cleared up. I'll tell you something though. That's the most original getaway excuse I've ever been offered.' For another half-hour, Mitchell took Jackson through the previous weekend, helping him to search his memory for scraps of confirmatory evidence from someone still alive. When the chairs became hard and uncomfortable they decided to adjourn to the Ring of Bells across the road. 'You might remember something when you're not trying.'

Resignedly, Jackson agreed. 'I'll have to do a final check of lights and doors in the church. I won't be long.'

Mitchell waited in the vestry until a noise of hammering and raised voices brought him to his feet. It became louder and clearer as he opened the door into the Lady chapel. The newcomer had entered by the organ door which Jackson had opened in answer to the importunate banging. Mitchell recognized the slim youth from his photograph. He was becoming hysterical, despite Jackson's efforts to soothe him.

'You killed those girls! I was there so you can't deny it. I won't tell anybody but I'm never going to have anything to do with you again!'

Mitchell arrived home after midnight to find his wife placidly reading a paperback novel. She laid it down and uncurled herself from her armchair. 'I'll make bacon sandwiches. Even I can't spoil those. You make coffee while I fry.' She cut short his apology for his late return. 'They all behaved beautifully for once. I've read more than half my book.'

Mitchell felt a tremendous sense of well-being as

the bacon spat under the grill, coffee dripped through the filter and his wife cut thick slices of bread. He described his day ruefully.

'Why did you go to see Barry Parker?'

'Well, Jennifer was talking to the daughter. Apparently she applied to be one of Marianne Baxter's tarts. She's better-looking than most, yet she was turned down.'

'She's not very discreet, perhaps.'

'Well, neither was Paula – but Parker's a ladies' man by all accounts, and he stopped having sexual relations with his daughter last year when he found he was carrying the can for sins that may not have been his, so he would have wanted his bit on the side from somewhere else. I was wondering if he was one of Marianne's customers, and whether she was scared that Stephanie and then his wife would find out. All he'd admit to was knowing Briony as Stephanie's friend but he gave me some useful background. Stephanie and Jonathan came to live with him because Jon had heard his mother saying she supposed she'd be lumbered with them both. He said Jon got adolescent and moody just as Debbie got pregnant with Benjie, the younger boy in the second family. Sad, isn't it, when a caring father is pulled so many ways and doesn't know what to do for the best.'

'The older boy must have been born whilst his mother was still just the mistress.'

'I suppose so. I asked for an account of his movements from Friday evening. It was like drawing teeth, though he was a bit more forthcoming when I suggested that little boys have good memories. He does seem genuinely fond of the younger kids.'

'So it was the organist who kept you?'

'Right. I thought it would be a quick chat till the boy turned up.'

'But not for long, I gather.'

'He shot off, probably because he saw me, whilst Jackson was still recovering from his accusation. We skipped the pub session. Jonathan was picked up by uniforms when he'd barely got out of the churchyard. Jackson volunteered to come down to the station to try to sort things out but as soon as we became involved the kid clammed up. Knew all about his right to silence. We asked Rory Jackson to come in. He was pretty upset both about his brother and the boy. We let Cavill go home but we're keeping Jonathan for his thirty-six hours. Jackson's trying to persuade him that an explanation from him is in everyone's best interests, but the lad's not used to the idea of the police on his side, or anyone else for that matter. He said we'd twist anything he said to make it look how we wanted. I wish I could have looked him in the eye and sworn we never did. Any more of that bacon?'

Virginia wrapped bread round the last two rashers and fetched him another bottle of her father's home-brew. 'When you're outside that, you should feel strong enough for today's study hour.'

Mitchell was horrified. 'What, at nearly one o'clock?'

'OK. Make it half an hour.' The telephone rang. Virginia was alarmed. 'It's got to be bad news at this hour. I hope no one's found any more bodies.' She lifted the receiver then handed it over. 'It's Jennifer for you.'

'Jennie?'

She did not reprove him for the diminutive. 'I know it's late but the station told me you hadn't been in long so I thought you wouldn't be asleep.'

'Cut the cackle. What's up?'

'I had a phone call earlier this evening from a girl I made friends with in training school in Wakefield. She moved down south after her two probationary years, but we keep in touch. On Sunday, I was telling her about our case, and she rang me tonight because she's found a book of cuttings in their archives.' Jennifer's suppressed excitement was beginning to transfer itself. 'In 1984 there was a triple murder in Cornwall, on the outskirts of St Austell. Three prostitutes, one still a schoolgirl, were strangled with some kind of a chain. The case is still open. They never found out exactly where the killings took place but the bodies were all brought to a bus shelter on a quiet road during the night and arranged on the bench seat to form an orderly queue.'

'Minus their handbags?'

'Minus their handbags.'

'What does my esteemed father-in-law say?'

'Unlike you, he went off duty at a respectable hour. He's probably asleep. I thought if it had waited thirteen years already it could wait until early in the morning.'

Mitchell related this latest development to his wife. After a lifetime in a police family, she was not greatly impressed. 'I said it would be more bodies. By the way, I've eaten the rest of your sandwich.'

On Wednesday morning, a flat battery made Browne twenty minutes late for his briefing. He paused in the corridor outside his door to catch his breath after running upstairs. He was not about to lose face for his lack of fitness as well as for the unprecedented discourtesy of keeping his men waiting. Trying to make his panting as nearly soundless as possible, he was glad to hear his son-in-law's voice in full flow.

'Have your money ready, ladies and gents. Are you going for the favourite or are you ready to live dangerously? Seven to four on the organist who gets all the dosh. Joint second favourites at two to one, the black guy who locked up the handbags or Barry Parker.'

'Why is he second favourite?' (Jennifer's voice.)

'Because he's a bastard and if we can't get him for what he's done to his daughter we'll have him for something else. He's probably had every one of the girls and he doesn't want his wife to find out. If you like a bit more of a risk, there's his lad. Three to one for him, I think. After all, he vamooshed, and anyway, he's an old customer of ours.'

Andy Craig had got into the spirit. 'Same odds for Ruth Roberts because I never trust a little goody-two-shoes.'

'What about Enright?' (Jennifer again.)

'Only eight to one for him. He's already sown his

wild oats and wants to settle down. The excitement would all be too much for him.'

Browne's ears pricked up. Had he heard the chink of coins? Suddenly he felt less amused. Mitchell's voice flowed on. 'For rank outsiders, we have one probation officer, one vicar, a collection of choirboys and one DCI. What's that? You wouldn't have believed it of him? But then, you wouldn't have believed he'd be late for his own briefing, would you?'

What better cue for an entry would he ever have, Browne asked himself. He pushed open his door, swept in and watched Mitchell's mouth fall open. He grinned at him. 'Thanks for holding the fort.' He swept up the pile of pound coins on his desk. 'I'll look after the stakes till the case breaks, and the winner can name his choice of charity. There's not much to discuss this morning. You'll all have heard of Jennifer's breakthrough. She and I will be off to St Austell to follow it up this morning. Keep studying the file. There'll be a short quiz later. No further notice given. Oh, and keep your reports up to date. Let's have you straight on the job. I want to know all about those handbags.'

He considered his three possible sources of information. 'Dez Mallett seems the most wimpish of the trio who could help us with them. Benny, get him in again and give him a hard time. Jennifer, I've seen your note on Mrs Staniforth. Before we set off for the deep south get on to the phone company again and see if they've checked yet whether Briony Cocker's call was long enough to be itemized. The next floor show will be in here at two. Have your entertainment ready,

Benny. It'll be Superintendent Petty who'll be selling tickets at the door.'

The telephone rang. Browne listened and held out the receiver to Jennifer. 'For you.' He ushered out the rest of the team then turned to see Jennifer's stricken face. 'What is it?' He pushed her into his chair but she immediately stood up again.

'It's Lucy's school. She's fallen from the climbing frame on to her head. They've taken her to the Infirmary.'

Browne wasted no time on sympathy. 'Off you go then. Want someone to drive you?'

She shook her head. 'No, I'm fine.' As she hurried out she collided with Mitchell coming back. His apology to his DCI died on his lips. 'What's up with her?'

Browne explained and added Jennifer's call to the telephone company to Mitchell's list of jobs. 'By the way, I'm not a killjoy, Benny, but next time don't play for money.' The phone rang again. Receiver in hand, Browne called Mitchell back. 'Jennifer's car's misbehaving as well as mine. Take her to the Infirmary. If Dez Mallett gets here before you get back, it'll give him time to get even more scared.'

Denis Betts, warden of St Barnabas', was almost as good as new but not yet ready to be sent back to his work. He had been deserted once more by his family so that the decorating could be resumed. Such activities had been expressly forbidden by the hospital, but he had decided that decorating with Irene away was marginally more restful than sitting about and listening to her reproaches.

He had awoken this morning, though, with an irresistible compulsion to visit old Mr Oliver. His conscience whispered that it was just an excuse, but he argued against it very stoutly. It was one of the things he could do to ease the burden on Tony, and where would any of his family have been this last week without the vicarage family?

His stitches had been taken out but Denis had been warned against driving just yet. Still, it was fine for once and now he felt really well for the first time in months, walking was a pleasure. On the half-mile to his destination, Denis was stopped no less than five times by people who asked after his health and wished him well. Grateful for the concern and the blessing of good friends, he determined to do his own bit to make the world a better place by being very patient with Mr Oliver, however crotchety he might be today.

Reaching the house, he noticed that the paintwork had been washed and the windows cleaned. If the Kirkbrides had not actually done the work, Denis was sure it had been done at their behest. He banged on the door and waited. He banged again and sighed. The old fool was probably having one of his deaf days where he heard everything much better the second time even if it was spoken more quietly. When the door remained shut after a third hammering, Denis felt ashamed. He hadn't been able to get to his own door last week, and look at the trouble the postman had taken over him.

As he contemplated the neatest way to break in, a voice spoke to him, closely followed by the appearance of a head over the hedge. 'He's not here, Denis. He's staying with his daughter. Went last Wednesday, same day as you were taken ill. It's given me a break from cooking his dinners.'

Denis blinked. 'Yes, it would do. Right, I'll get back then.' He trudged back slowly. No respite from the wallpapering now.

Mitchell showed his solidarity with Jennifer by silently concentrating on fast, safe driving. When she declined his offer to escort her into the hospital building, he saluted and left her. With some of her tasks shunted to his own list, his morning promised to be even busier than he had expected, but the novelty and cheerfulness of the powerless sunshine tempted him to drive round three sides of the park on the way back to the station.

As he approached the main entrance, he saw a man struggling a little to restrain a large dog on a leash. It was a mongrel but a fine, spirited animal. As he caught up with it, Mitchell realized that the man it was dragging along with it was Cavill Jackson. He stopped the car and climbed out to pass the time of day. So often, useful information was obtained when a witness or suspect was off guard.

Jackson was breathlessly cheerful. 'Meet Bonzo. He's Rory's. I don't know if he's missed him yet. I found him making for the park as I was going home from playing at the midweek Communion. I took him in there and gave him a good chase because I'll have to shut him up now till Rory can collect him.'

'I didn't see him when I called on your brother.'

'He'd probably run off then too. He escapes more days than he doesn't. Fortunately, they have better control over their children.' He rubbed his hand where the chain was biting and unwound it gingerly. 'The handle's come off this thing, so I have to wind the end of the chain twice round to get a grip.'

He rewound the chain on to his uninjured left hand and surveyed his painful right one ruefully.

'I would have expected a musician to take better care of his hands.'

'Oh, it doesn't do to get paranoid about these things.' Jackson massaged the angry red weals gently and flexed his hand. Mitchell looked on sympathetically, then froze. There in Jackson's firm flesh was the exact pattern that had been carefully sketched in the path lab and sent along with the PM reports. He had first seen it four days ago and fourfold, on the necks of the dead girls. He felt a great disappointment.

He realized that Jackson too was staring fixedly at his hand. The loosened grip of the other had given the dog its freedom again and it was cavorting along the pavement, dragging the chain and scattering pedestrians. 'This was very careless of you, Mr Jackson – unless you were wanting to give yourself up.'

There was a long silence before Jackson's reply. 'I didn't think I'd be meeting you.'

Following the gut judgement that rarely let him down, Mitchell kept the arrest low-key. He offered the statutory warning but used no restraints on his prisoner and let him ride beside him in the front of the car. It was a silent journey but, as the pair walked from the car to the foyer of the station, Jackson asked, 'I can have a phone call, can't I?'

'Possibly. Who are you wanting to ring?'

'I'd like to speak to Tony.'

'Mr Kirkbride?' He nodded. Mitchell shook his head. 'We've done away with capital punishment, you know. You don't need a priest. You'd do better with a good lawyer later on if it comes to a charge. Or what about your brother, for now? And he can't have his dog lead back, by the way.'

Jackson looked alarmed. 'It . . . er . . . isn't his. It's an old one that . . . that I don't use any more.'

'It seems to have had considerable use made of it this week, Mr Jackson.' Mitchell handed his prisoner over to the custody sergeant and went to report his return. He was depressed and plunged into his next task to distract himself. A case was never finished until a charge was brought, and the matter of the handbags still had to be followed up.

He didn't think Dez Mallett would take much breaking and he was soon proved right. Sobbing and snivelling, Dez admitted that Cracker had found the bags on Saturday night after they had brought in their latest haul from Crossley Bridge. Sola had not been there. He'd been busy in Kingsgate on Saturday evening.

'Had he now?'

Mallett was slightly cheered by the chance to put Sola at the scene of the more serious crime. He elaborated on the method they used and exactly what Sola might have been doing. 'We knock on doors and ask people to sign a petition, and we ask when any other people will be coming home so they can sign it as well, and then we know when it'll be safe.'

'Yes, I get the general idea. So Ogunade would have knocked at number seven and asked when all the girls would be in or out?'

Dez nodded complacently. Returning to his original tale he recounted how he had found Cracker rifling the bags and how he had reluctantly agreed to share the money with him.

'How much?'

Mallett looked sulky. 'My share was two-fifty.'

'Hell's teeth!' Could the girls just have been mugged for their money? The killer would still have to be crazy to have risked bringing the bodies to one place. One other little mystery was cleared up though. Uniforms had searched the Malletts' house and found a cheap but brand-new music centre. When challenged, Dez had produced the receipt for it. Now all was explained. 'So you threw the bags into the shed behind all the other stuff?' Dez nodded.

Presumably Jackson would have collected them later if it had not been for the coincidence of the police finding them whilst on the track of another set of villains. The allotments were lonely at night yet conveniently near to his house – and less potentially dangerous than hiding things under his pillow or in the church.

Mitchell told Dez he was free to go. When he

demanded a lift home, he admired the lad's effrontery and drove him there.

When Mitchell got back to the incident room, he found Jennifer at her desk. In answer to his enquiries, she told him that Lucy was sleeping. 'The X-ray revealed a hairline fracture but they don't seem to think any serious damage has been done. They're keeping her in for observation for a while longer. They'll ring me if she's distressed when she wakes up. Otherwise, I'm to visit late this afternoon. I've got no joy from the telephone people.'

'So what are all these?' Mitchell pointed to a page of jottings on the desk.

'This is from Yorkshire Television. Dora Staniforth said Briony was interested in what she was watching before she made her call. It was the local news. I haven't been able to find anyone who remembers exactly what was on, so I rang them to ask what they put out that night. I've starred what I thought might be relevant.'

She handed him the paper. Tony Kirkbride was starred as item 4, champion of small shopkeepers against the council. 'Oh yes, the new supermarket. There was a bit of a demo earlier on last week. Kev Collins got a black eye at it. Why have you starred this Doncaster choir?'

'Because that's where Briony Cocker comes from. From what I've heard about her, their programmes don't sound like her cup of tea, but I suppose she could have been at school with one of the singers or something.'

'This Bradford student, Ed Costello, sounds more promising. Aren't we supposed to be looking for an Edward? What's he done to get into the news?'

'Threatened to sue his tutors because they dismissed him from his course.'

'Why?'

'Because he's into sport in a big way and he's attended less than half his lectures and classes all year.'

Mitchell handed back the paper. 'It's probably all useless, Jen. We banged up Cavill Jackson this morning.'

'What for?'

Mitchell explained. 'I wish it hadn't been me who brought him in.'

'So, what's he got to say?'

'Not a lot. He's screaming for his vicar.'

Jennifer laughed. 'That'll be a first. We haven't had Regina versus the Power of Prayer before. Anyway, how does he know the vicar's on his side? Didn't you say Kirkbride thought he could have done it if his career was threatened?'

Mitchell shrugged. 'The Super told me it was all right to send for him, at any rate. Perhaps Petty thinks he'll advise Jackson to make a clean breast of everything. I got his wife when I rang. She said he was out but she'd try to contact him and pass the message on. In the meantime, I'll go and see if he's setting his defence to music.'

*

Tony Kirkbride had gone, as usual, from his midweek Communion service in church to take Sick Communion to the two ex-members of St Barnabas' who were more or less permanent residents in the geriatric ward at Cloughton Infirmary. One was duly grateful and thanked him with her customary courtesy. The other seemed hardly to recognize him but obviously drew comfort from the familiar ceremony.

His duties completed, he called in at the chaplain's office, partly as a courtesy but chiefly because he liked the man. There was a token discussion on the well-being of various patients from the parish, before the five minutes over a cup of coffee which was all they allowed themselves to continue their running argument concerning the ordination of women.

As Kirkbride was leaving, the chaplain took a scrap of paper from a desk drawer. 'I've got a message for you, though I'm not sure you'll know what to make of it. It's from a Mrs Dorothy Greenhow and it's just an Old Testament reference. Sadly, she died yesterday. I was speaking with her on Monday. She maintained that the Methodists know the Scriptures better than we Anglicans, and bet me that you'd have to look it up.'

'She probably had a point, but I'm surprised at the betting. I thought the Methodists were hot against it.' He reached for the paper with some trepidation. Had the old lady spoken to her unfortunate changeling and would he make anything of her cryptic message? There was just the stark reference in the chaplain's neat, italic script. *2nd Samuel 12. 7a.* He looked up. 'Isn't

Second Samuel Twelve Nathan the prophet, reproving David for pinching Uriah's wife? I'm not sure I can quote the exact verse.'

The chaplain grinned. 'You haven't been kissing the nurses, have you, under Mrs G.'s reproving eye? Anyway, I reckon you've maintained the honour of the Anglicans by knowing what's in the chapter. I looked the verse up for you – vulgar curiosity, I'm afraid.' He handed over a second slip of paper. '*Do* you know what she means?'

Kirkbride's voice was faint. 'I think so.' He leaned back against the wall and closed his eyes.

Concerned, the chaplain came over to him and took his arm. 'Was she a relation of yours? I'm sorry, I'd no idea. Look, sit down.'

Kirkbride shook off the arm. 'No, I was just fond of her. Could I just be alone in the chapel for a few minutes?' To reiterations of 'By all means', he managed to walk the fifteen or so yards up the corridor and sank down on the back row of chapel chairs.

Detective Constable Craig found Jennifer and Mitchell in the canteen. 'Magic's got a hysterical woman in the foyer, Kirkbride's wife. He says that sort of thing is women's work and where are you?'

Mitchell glanced at Craig warningly, then at Jennifer with trepidation. She grinned. 'Fine. Let's see what it is she's excited about.' She drained her coffee cup and left Mitchell to finish his second breakfast.

Mrs Kirkbride's indignation was signalled by

quivering chins over a quivering bosom. She continued her tirade without pause, merely transferring her glare to Jennifer from Magic. 'Out on this freezing-cold morning with hardly a stitch on. Jumper sleeves up to his elbows, hole in the knee of his jeans. Chasing that huge dog of Rory's!' So, Cavill Jackson was her current subject.

'Don't know how he can afford to feed it with three kiddies to keep. Cavill would never do anybody any harm, you know. Look at him with all those little boys! Takes them to concerts, takes them to the coast every summer, gives free music lessons to that naughty boy that Rory brought him. You've got it all wrong, you know.'

By now, Jennifer had steered her into Browne's office and seated her in his visitors' chair. 'Cavill wouldn't hurt a fly and now he needs Tony and we can't find him. Staff Nurse says he left Ward Eight ages ago, and he did say he might go and see Mr Oliver, but he can't have. I saw Denis Betts this morning and he told me Mr Oliver's not there. Gone to stay with his daughter.

'She must have been shamed into taking a bit of notice of him at last. Went last Wednesday, Denis says, but that can't be right because Tony was there on Friday night and said he'd go again this week.

'I wondered what I'd done wrong because he usually leaves Mr O. to me and Denis. Not that the old beggar'll be grateful. More than likely deny that Tony was there at all. I wish he'd come. I left a message with Sister to send him on if she saw him. And his car is still parked in the hospital grounds.'

'What sort of car is it?'

'Does it matter?' Jennifer nodded. 'It's a 325 estate, a BMW, a dark-red one. Do you think it would help Cavill at all to talk to me?'

Deciding this was the last thing Jackson needed, Jennifer offered her witness a cup of coffee and rang for Caroline to bring it.

Having drawn at least two breaths, Jean Kirkbride had set off on another verbal ramble. 'Funny about Tony and hospitals.'

'Is it?'

'Yes, Tony has a vicar friend who always seems to get parishes with a church school. With Tony, it's hospitals. Of course, they have their own chaplains now, but when we were down in Truro it was half Tony's job to be hospital chaplain and the parish was very small to make up for it.'

'My boss is down in that area today . . .' Jennifer was thinking furiously. 'How many miles is Truro from St Austell?'

Jean shook her head. 'I couldn't tell you exactly, but not far at all.'

'When were you there?'

'We went in seventy-eight. Tony liked it so we stayed eight years.'

Caroline knocked and came in with the coffee. Jennifer smiled at her. 'Could you look after Mrs Kirkbride for a minute? I just have to speak to Sergeant Mitchell.

Did you say that your husband was going to see Mr Oliver today?'

Jean looked impatient. 'Well, he can't, can he? Mr Oliver isn't there but Tony doesn't know that . . .' Jennifer had gone. Caroline blinked as her heels clattered down the corridor.

Jennifer caught Mitchell as he was leaving the canteen and pulled him back to a table there. She summarized quickly what Jean Kirkbride had told her. 'They were in Cornwall in 1984, only a few miles from St Austell. He told lies about where he was on Friday night, thinking he was safe because the old man couldn't remember who had been to see him. He appeared in the TV news that Briony Cocker was watching before she made her telephone call. What if Kirkbride was one of Marianne's clients and Briony had just found out he was a vicar? He'd have to stop her telling the others. Maybe the others were killed because she'd spoken to them already.'

Jennifer's voice rose suddenly, in panic. 'And Mr Oliver's the alibi he's using. Jean Kirkbride says that's where he's going after the hospital, so what's he up to right now?'

'I'll see Petty right away.' Mitchell leaped up and set off, then turned back. 'What about Jackson and the dog chain? Ask Jean Kirkbride about that, will you?' He was gone, leaving Jennifer wondering how fourteen stones of him could move so rapidly and soundlessly. She gave herself a mental kick. How had Jean Kirkbride known about Cavill and the dog? She must have met him before Benny had. And *Cavill*

Jackson had no dog, so where did the lead come from? The Kirkbrides' car? So that was why Jackson had arrived at the police station demanding to see his priest!

Tony Kirkbride concentrated on his surroundings, trying to push his new knowledge out of his mind. He could not cope yet with all its implications. He stared at the square block of the Communion table with its artistically rough-hewn board on top, then rested his eyes on the ecclesiastical blue of the furnishings. Why were they always blue? He gazed at the grey walls with their flower prints. No holy pictures, thank God. This was no mental blasphemy.

He focused on a tall triangle of flowers on its wrought-iron stand, then laid his forearm along the backs of the chairs in front of him and rested his head on it in an attitude of prayer. The words of Dorothy's message burned into the darkness behind his closed lids. *And Nathan said unto David, 'Thou art the man'.*

He was the man who had grown from that baby, stolen from his prostitute mother, given to Alice Kirkbride, who was not his mother, who had pushed him into the Church, kept him in her subjection with the expectation of his inheritance. Imbued as she was with her sense of 'family', her horror at this revelation might even exceed his own.

She would never have contemplated adoption, even by conventional and respectable means. Dorothy had very likely intended to keep her secret till Alice was dead, till her revelation would not have meant him forfeiting the estate he had grown up to expect would be his. It should have happened that way. Alice was older.

He could see that she had meant so well, had had no conception of the tragedy she had caused his life to become. But there was no excuse for her, whatever the circumstances, however many bombs had fallen round her as she made her decision to interfere in the natural course of events. What had he told her? That he did not believe in a God who punished mistakes that were made from pure motives. He had thought his words to be perfectly true, because he did not believe in a God at all. Now, he was not so sure. He must believe in God to be so angry with him. To blame him because the woman he had loved, no, idolized, was not his sister. He was not a pervert. Those low-born women on whom he had been obliged to sate his bodily appetites had died for nothing. But it wasn't God's fault, it was Dorothy's.

He fell on his knees, welcoming the discomfort of the bare wooden floorboards. In an undertone, he repeated the Lord's Prayer, drawing ragged breaths between the phrases and finishing, as in the old Evensong, before the doxology. 'Deliver us from evil.' Dorothy had delivered him in every sense, and the evil from which she had delivered him would have been better for him by far than the good life she had thought she was bestowing on him.

After a time, his trembling stilled. Soon, when he felt real again, when he could feel his feet on the ground again, he would go home, tell Jean she could go back to being his housekeeper. He would take down his photographs and tear them up. He would throw away those shoddy handbags. He would drive to his mother's – no, to Alice Kirkbride's – house and tell Diana . . .

'Tony.' The chaplain stood in the doorway of the chapel, looking shocked himself. 'Can you come out? There are some policemen to see you.'

Jennifer Taylor parked her Fiesta neatly in a free corner of the hospital car park. She locked it and paused to consider the chipped paint on the bonnet, where the stone kicked by Andy Craig had struck it. She realized that she felt no indignation, that she was merely putting off entering the building and having her fears confirmed.

In normal circumstances, Lucy was a well-adjusted, sociable child and very happy to be minded by Granny Jane. An injured and frightened little girl, though, needed her mother. Lucy, however tough, was only five years old. She had had to make do with a visit from her grandmother this afternoon and now Jennifer was late for the evening visit she had promised to make herself. Taking the Reverend Anthony Kirkbride into custody and completing the paperwork that this entailed had seemed to last for ever. If she failed to persuade the staff nurse to allow her to stay beyond the official end of visiting, Jennifer would have barely ten minutes to spend with her daughter. It was just not fair to press on with her career at the expense of the well-being of her two small children.

She opened the ward door and entered pandemonium. Two young boys wrestled on a mat, knocking against a table at which two smaller children were trying to complete a jigsaw puzzle. The annoyed shrieks of one of them rivalled those of two little girls who were using the beds in the far corner as trampolines, leaping incredible heights above the mattresses. The bed where Lucy had been sleeping was empty. Jennifer was not surprised. Her daughter had probably been moved to a side ward where she could rest undisturbed.

Jennifer had turned to enquire of a nurse where she should go, when she heard herself being greeted enthusiastically. 'Look, Mum. I can jump much higher than Samira!' The leaping continued for some seconds as Samira rose to the challenge in every sense. Waist-length black hair flew round both heads. Then, Lucy landed neatly on her bottom, rocking as the bed springs continued to vibrate and the mattress to rise and fall. 'You haven't come to fetch me home yet, have you? I like it here.'

DC Chris Winters smiled at his female companion across the restaurant table. She stopped chewing, swallowed and demanded to know what was amusing him.

'Well, whenever Andy Craig and I have worked together on a case before, he's been the one to pick up a girlfriend as part of the deal. Usually, I've been pleased to let him. Andy's kind of girl holds no attractions for me. This time, he's lost out.'

'Is he the one who looks like a young Bob Geldof?' Winters nodded. 'No he hasn't, then. I was in the Green Dragon last night with some friends and I saw DC Craig with a dyed blonde. He introduced her, but I already knew her.' She paused to provoke him.

Winters reviewed the cast of suspects and witnesses he had interviewed, discussed or read about in the file during the past ten days. 'Stephanie Parker?' He smiled to himself. The pairings seemed almost too neat. But Craig was just running true to form, whereas for himself, something unusual and irrevocable was happening.

'Got it in one. All I need now is to see James wining and dining someone. Then I'll stop feeling so guilty.'

Winters sighed. 'You're not one of those women who always have to be agonizing over something?'

Ruth Roberts considered the question. 'Do you know, I'm rather afraid I might be.'

'Well, if you have to worry, worry about the amount of his life you've wasted by being the wrong woman for him.' He watched her arrange her knife and fork neatly across the diameter of her empty plate. 'I don't think your anxiety's terminal. It hasn't spoiled your appetite.'

Benjie Parker stuffed his hymn book haphazardly into his pigeon-hole in the choir vestry after Friday practice. He was concluding yet another argument with his brother. This time he easily managed to have the last word, even though it was spoken quite audibly. 'Told you in the park she was the vicar's girlfriend. She was so!'

Jon Parker sat on the stool of the St Barnabas organ and glared at his recalcitrant feet.

'Your boots are too big,' said a voice from behind him. 'Take them off and try again.'

Jon attempted the foot-pedal exercise bootless, with rather more success. 'Once more.' Jon groaned but obeyed. 'Right. Now you're ready for your first piece of organ music proper.' It was a struggle but Jon managed it at a rather slower tempo than was set.

Cavill Jackson saw that the boy had had enough and brought his lesson to an end. 'Now your course is finished, and until you get a job, we might fit in an extra lesson after the service on Wednesday mornings, and a couple of extra practice sessions.' Jon's face lit up. 'I'll see Mr Betts, the warden, and arrange for the church to be open for us. Now off you go. I've some things of my own to practise.' The youth lingered. 'No, you can't listen. It'll just be the difficult bits, over and over.' Still he did not go. Jackson sighed. 'What is it?'

'Cav, on that Saturday, I never really thought you could have . . . but . . . I was up the tree and I didn't see who else . . . When the vicar left, he waved goodbye, so I thought they must have been alive then, and—'

'Jon, it's all right. Scram! You're using up my practice time.'

'Can I turn the pages for you?'

'Not tonight, no. By the way, have you got a passport?'

'No. Why?'

'I'll be playing the two sorties in Madrid since they went down so well in Cologne. I shall want a page-turner there who knows the music and the way I play it.'

Jon's voice was wistful. 'I'd love to, but there's no way I could afford it.'

'I'm offering you a job, man, not a pleasure trip. There'll be more to do than just that.'

Jackson noted, as the lad loped off down the aisle, that the hunch of his shoulders had disappeared as well as the droop at the mouth. When the interregnum was over, perhaps the new vicar could be persuaded that, in view of his own overseas commitments, it would be a good idea to appoint a young boy as assistant organist.

Diana Kirkbride stared, unseeing, at her well-preserved face in her dressing-table mirror and contemplated with respect her mother's continuing command both of herself and of her family. Kathleen, the housekeeper, had announced Jean's arrival and Diana had found herself dismissed, sent to amuse herself as though she were a child, whilst her mother settled a grown-up's problem.

The formerly unflappable Kathleen was having trouble adapting to the new circumstances. 'Mrs . . . er, Miss . . . er, Jean Johnson is here.'

So, Jean had gone back to her maiden name. She would probably be much more comfortable with it – and more comfortable minding and caring for the vicarage in Tony's absence than she had been during her uneasy year as his wife. Diana had certainly found Jean more relaxed in her own dealings with her in the last few weeks.

She wondered how the two women downstairs were getting on with their business. Her lack of resentment at being banished was because she knew the substance of Jean's news, had been consulted about her mother's capacity to bear it . . . Having stoically accepted that her much-loved son was the killer of seven young girls, Alice was now about to learn that the unconsummated marriage between Jean and Tony was to be annulled.

At least her mother had been spared the further shock that Tony had planned for her. He had seen the murder of seven young girls as no bar to his own marriage to herself, even suggesting that it would be a comfort to Alice, who had lost him as her son, to regain him as her son-in-law. He had been very angry when she turned down his proposal and now he was refusing to see her.

Diana was grateful for the respite in which she could consider whether any relationship between them was possible in the future. Not the one he had in mind, naturally, but perhaps they would write to each other.

*

The hospital chaplain had not been looking forward to visiting Alice Kirkbride. However, he felt he should offer his condolences and see whether there was anything he could do for her. He was not sure that she would receive him. He was not family. She might tell him, very politely, to mind his own business.

He found though that Alice was anxious to speak to him, to anyone in fact who could tell her what had happened to her son. And the chaplain was the only visitor, so far, whom Tony had been prepared to receive. At his request, he had heard Tony's confession, then offered him the luxury of a non-judgemental listener to his less confidential explanations.

The chaplain attempted to convey to Alice the substance of these latter revelations. 'Yes, he could understand that the preservation of his own good name was no justification for killing all those people, but he'd been brought up to have a very strong sense of family. He felt he must guard its reputation.' Alice nodded approvingly. 'Of course, he was ashamed on his own account for what he called his "regrettable association with prostitutes". In his tortured mind, though, getting rid of the girls he had defiled somehow removed his sense of the injury he had done them.'

'He thinks adultery is wrong but murder is all right.' Alice made an inimitable gesture. 'Well, of course, we know now that he was not actually a Kirkbride.'

The delicious casserole being dispensed at the Mitchells' kitchen table had been prepared by Benny.

Virginia had been left to switch on the oven at the appropriate time and had managed not to spoil it. She faced him across their two steaming plates.

'Benny, there's something we need to discuss. The O'Brien blood in you won't like it.' Mitchell knew what was coming. Was surprised the matter had not been raised before. 'I intend – well, would like – to make sure there aren't any more children.'

'Right.'

'So, what do you think?'

'I said right.'

'Aren't we going to talk about it?'

'We have. And now I've got my hour's studying to do. You're already the Chief Inspector's daughter. I'm giving myself five years to make you the Chief Inspector's wife.'